Snowbound

Kit Kyndall

Published by Amourisa Press, 2015.

Kit Tunstall, writing as Kit Kyndall, reserves all rights to Snowbound. Any resemblance to people or places is a coincidence. Please respect the copyright by not sharing this work. Permission of the author or publisher is required to copy any part of this work. All sexually active characters depicted in this work of fiction are 18 years of age or older.

© Kit Tunstall, 2014

Cover images courtesy of Depositphotos.com

Join Kit's Mailing List[1] (www.kittunstall.com/newsletter) to receive notification of new releases and access bonus chapters for your favorite books. You get six free books just for signing up—and I'll tell you how to read my books before anyone else, and for less! If you prefer to receive notifications for just one, or a few, of Kit's pen names, you'll have the option to select which lists to subscribe to at signup.

---

1. http://kittunstall.com/newsletter/

Blurb

PLANNING TO SURPRISE her father, Beth Wyndam arrives at Reed Nixon's Alaskan guide facility a day earlier than the rest of her party. Terrible weather snows her in with the surly older man, but she finds herself drawn to him despite his grumpiness. Reed wants her too, but the fifteen years separating them, along with the differences in their backgrounds, are obstacles he can't bring himself to ignore. With a little luck, a lot of snow, and a power outage, Beth gets Reed in her bed. It's everything she had hoped, but the real challenge is not falling in love with a man who warned from the start there was no future for them—especially when she realizes there will be a permanent reminder of their affair.

Chapter One

REED NIXON WAS IN A foul mood, and he had no trouble admitting it. His coffeepot had broken that morning, and it was a damned pain in the ass to replace, living way up north. He'd have to special order it, have it shipped to Fairbanks, and then delivered via a charter company to Endline. After that, he'd have to drive two hundred miles down Dalton Highway in his rugged SUV, and that was a trip he hadn't planned on for at least another three months, until after the last of the worst weather passed for the season.

On top of that, he'd discovered a hole in his favorite snow boots, and one of the strings on his crossbow—that had cost almost as much as the SUV—was fraying, necessitating changing, which could be a time-consuming process, even for someone who knew a crossbow inside and out.

So, the last thing he felt like was greeting his arriving clients early. The Wyndam party wasn't scheduled to arrive until tomorrow. He'd been toying with the idea of contacting the charter service to see if his pal Mike was flying in the guests. If so, he'd planned to ask Mike to bring him any kind of coffee machine, as long as it dispensed the thick, dark, and hot drink he needed to feel semi-human of a morning.

Knowing that wasn't happening was part of the reason he was so surly as he shrugged on his coat and boots, stomping through the snow to the airfield he'd had put in a few years ago, when he'd launched his guide business. He'd be the first to acknowledge that he was generally surly anyway, as a rule.

When the small plane landed, he threw up his hands, waiting until the door opened, and the stairs descended. "I wasn't expecting you until tomorrow, Wyndam," he started to snarl. His mouth snapped shut for just a minute as a petite figure in a bulky white parka and cumbersome white snow boots stepped down the stairs carefully.

As she drew nearer, he demanded, "Who the hell are you? Wyndam told me it'd be just him and his camera crew. He didn't say nothin' about his girlfriend comin' along." She flinched at the rough tone, and he felt a spark of regret when he noticed how young she was. That fled when she opened her mouth.

"I'm his daughter, not his girlfriend, and who the hell are you?" She asked the question in exactly the same tone he had. "Daddy said the tour guide would meet me, but that can't be you."

Her dismissive look rose his hackles—and brought back some of his old insecurities from growing up dirt-poor and the son of the town drunk. "Why can't that be me, sweetheart?" He practically snarled the question at her.

If she was at all intimidated, it didn't show. "Someone getting paid to take care of a group wouldn't be so unprofessional."

He opened his mouth, but then shut it for a moment, deciding she had a point. "I'm sorry," he said, still gruffly. "I wasn't expecting nobody 'til tomorrow."

She nodded. "I guess you needed that extra twenty-four hours to find your manners, huh?"

Just like that, the little hellion set his teeth back on-edge. In an attempt to control his irritation, he walked to the pilot, who wasn't Mike. He thought this one was Vic, who mainly flew charters out of Fairbanks. "Vic?" At the man's nod, he held out his hand, more to show the irritating kitten beside him that he had some manners than because he actually felt compelled to make a friendly greeting. "How're you doin'?" After a quick exchange of pleasantries, he asked, "Where's the rest of 'em?"

Vic shrugged. "Don't know. Got a call asking us to fly in Ms. Wyndam today, and still plan on bringing the rest tomorrow."

With a small sigh, he turned back to face the young woman. "Ms. Wyndam, where is the rest of your party?"

She gave him a sweet smile, but her green eyes still crackled with banked anger. "They're still in Endline and planning to come tomorrow, as scheduled. I happened to arrive early, so Daddy arranged for the charter company to pick me up in Fairbanks and deliver me here."

He nodded just once. "Well, where's your gear?" He expected to be hauling suitcases into the guest quarters for the next hour, so it was a bit of a surprise to have Vic hand him just one large suitcase. "You just staying overnight?" he joked, as he lifted the suitcase, bade Vic goodbye, and led the girl—young woman—toward the guest quarters.

She frowned. "No, I'm here for a couple of weeks. Why?"

He lifted the bag a bit higher. "Most women I've seen come here," and he could count the number on one hand, "Bring a mountain of luggage."

"Oh. Daddy mentioned he was packing light, but bringing lots of warm things." Her smile seemed genuine. "I have to warn you that my dad's idea of light packing is a lot different than mine."

He waved a hand. "A girl who listens to her father. That's unusual in your generation."

She rolled her eyes. "My generation? What are you, ten minutes older than me?"

A genuine laugh burst from him. "Sweetheart, I'm thirty-three."

As he opened the door that allowed the guests their own private entrance and exit, he moved aside to let her pass. She paused right in front of him, leaning against the doorway for a moment in her puffy white parka. "Well, sweetheart, I'm eighteen. That's hardly another generation."

She slipped on past him, turning back to look over her shoulder as she added, "And I only listen to my father when I feel like it."

Feeling slightly bemused, he followed her into his house, quickly overtaking her shorter stride, to give her the brief tour. "This is the guests' quarters. There are two rooms. A small private room, and a larger room with six bunks." He gestured to a door nearby. "You go through there for the commode." Farther down the wood-paneled hall, he pointed to another door. "That leads to the kitchen. It's shared space with my residence, but you're welcome to help yourself to anything. I hope your daddy told you to bring any special thing you wanted along. I keep the basics, and then some, but I don't offer no fancy stuff."

"Darn," she said with a small hint of mocking. "I guess I should have packed champagne and caviar instead of my pants."

The idea of this young woman running around in no pants caused a sudden hitch in his breathing. He didn't reply to the sarcasm as he led her to the small private room with its double bed. "You'll have to make do with this. I laid out toiletries for a man, expecting Mr. Wyndam to stay in this room. He didn't say nothin' about a girl," he reminded.

"Yeah, I know. Daddy isn't one for bragging about his children." She said it offhandedly, as though it was no big deal, but he thought there was a hint of hurt underneath. Or maybe he was just projecting his own rotten childhood onto her.

He set her bag down on the trunk at the foot of the bed, near the rustic log footboard he'd made himself. "I'll leave you to unpack, Ms. Wyndam. I fix dinner around six, unless you prefer to look after yourself." He wanted to scoff at the thought. It seemed clear to him that the little princess in front of him wasn't used to doing much for herself. Apparently, making documentaries was a lot more lucrative than he'd ever imagined, judging from her appearance and demeanor. He knew for a fact the coat she wore cost several thousand dollars. He had one from the same designer, but it was their Outlet line, and he'd had to save three years to afford it. Of course, he'd never need another one. Point was, quality costs, and she'd clearly paid a lot. Well, her Daddy's Amex had, he thought, with a grimace of distaste.

She smiled. "Thank you, Mr....?"

"Reed."

"Mr. Reed."

He shook his head, sending shaggy brown strands falling into his eyes. "Nah, just Reed. Reed Nixon."

She chose that moment to push back the hood of her parka and take off the soft-looking light-pink hat underneath. A mass of silvery-blonde hair fell free, and even the confining ponytail couldn't keep all the determined strands tamed. He had the insane urge to bury his hand in the tresses and tug her closer. Thankfully, it was a notion that passed quickly, and he took a step back to make sure he didn't do anything asinine.

"Well, thanks, just Reed. I'm Beth." She stripped off her gloves before tackling the zipper. "Goodness, my fingers are frozen," she said. Struggling with the coat, she looked disconcertingly like a little girl for a moment.

Reed stepped quickly to the door. "I'll get a fire started in the common area. Just through that door, same as the kitchen." Without awaiting a response, he ducked out of the room and back into his own quarters. It took every ounce of self-control not to bolt the door that separated his house from the guestrooms, as though he could lock out his unexpected reaction by keeping the door between them barred.

"You're losin' it, man," he said softly to himself, as he went to build up the fire that was little more than a smoldering crackle at the moment.

Beth didn't believe in love at first sight. That was nonsense you read about in romance books, or saw in movies. She certainly hadn't fallen for Reed Nixon on sight. He'd been surly and short-tempered, and not at all charming or warm. Nope, definitely not on sight. As she brushed out her hair and smoothed down her sweater, nerves made her stomach jump, and she tried to decide at what point she'd fallen in lust—not love—with the grouchy guide.

Her lips twitched as she remembered the pointed way he'd shaken the pilot's hand. The only thing missing had been him sticking his tongue out at her and saying, "Neener, neener, neener." Yeah, that was about the time she'd realized there was more to him than just a grump.

His voice was deep and rough, with a rich southern twang that seemed a little out of place in the Far North region. She liked it though, and it didn't take too much imagination to have him whispering all sorts of naughty things in her head as she got ready to join him for dinner.

Leaning forward to touch up her lip-gloss, she met her own eyes in the mirror and grinned. He'd be the type to speak plainly, and probably earthily, rather than vaguely or whimsically. She had a feeling Reed was the kind of man who would tell a woman he wanted to fuck her, instead of asking to make love to her.

Considering the boys she knew—and none of them could be counted as men when compared to Reed—were all the romance and flowers type, she thought it would be refreshing to have a real man telling her bluntly what he wanted her to do. Or do to her, she imagined with a small shiver.

Of course, she had to get him to notice her as more than a paying client's daughter first. It was obvious he considered her a little girl, and a real man had no interest in little girls.

A quick glance at the gold watch on her wrist revealed it was five until six, so she slipped out of the room and down the hall. Pausing at the door, she took one more deep breath for courage before opening it to enter the common area.

She let her gaze dance around the interior, finding it was more paneled wood, rustic timber supports, and some type of white stone accents. There was a large fur on the floor near the fireplace, and she frowned at it. She knew Reed ran a guide business, and that included taking clients out to hunt, but she didn't approve. Thankfully, her daddy wasn't one of those idiot outdoorsmen, preferring to do his shooting with a camera instead of a gun. He was here to make a documentary on the wildlife of the Far North.

The small great room led right into the kitchen, which held a dining table big enough for eight. She paused to admire the raw log legs before running a hand over the smooth wood. "This is pretty. Where'd you get it?"

He looked up from the stove for the first time since she entered the room, though she was positive he'd seen her the moment she opened the door from the guest quarters.

"I made it myself. Pretty much have to if you want something out here."

So, he had skilled hands. That thought made her tingle between the thighs, and she pressed them together discreetly. "Can I help with anything?"

He looked surprised by the offer, along with more than a tad disbelieving. "Nah, I got it. Just some stew and cornbread."

She nodded, taking a seat beside the chair at the head of the table, which she correctly assumed would be his. He didn't seem to like her proximity, and she had a moment of doubt. Could she really get this man to see her as a woman, not just an inconvenient adolescent?

He set a big bowl of stew down, along with a basket of cornbread. She was a little surprised to find he'd wrapped the bread in a red-checked cloth. He was so male, so raw and rough, that she wouldn't have been surprised if he'd served the stew in the pot and the cornbread still in the pan.

She helped herself to some of both and spooned up a bite of the stew. "Wow, this is good. What brand is it?"

He blinked. "Brand?"

Beth arched a brow. "You know, like what company put it in the can?"

Reed made a scoffing sound. "Ain't no can, girl. I made it. Like I said, you want something in this environment, you gotta know how to make it." He gave her an unreadable look. "Lot of folks like comin' here for trips and such, but they ain't got what you need to survive out here."

She bristled at the implication she wasn't tough or able to make do. Just because she never had didn't mean she couldn't. Still, arguing with him seemed counterproductive to trying to seduce him, so she bit her tongue. Her seduction plans were looking less likely with every passing minute though. Her dad and the film crew would be joining them tomorrow, and she doubted there'd be any opportunities after that.

"Well, it's delicious. What's in it?"

If he found the question as stupid as it was, he was nice enough not to be too obvious. "Potatoes, carrots, onions, garlic, gravy, and caribou."

She frowned, putting down her spoon. "Caribou?"

He nodded. "You got a problem with that? You seemed to be enjoyin' it a moment ago."

Beth grimaced. "I don't approve of hunting when there's food in the grocery store."

Reed laughed, and it was more than a bit mocking. "Where'd you think that food comes from, girl? The cow fairy?"

She frowned. "I'm not a girl, and I know where it comes from. Those animals are raised in captivity. They wouldn't know how to survive if you set them free, unlike the wildlife."

He snorted. "So you're doing a favor by killing them?" He didn't wait for a reply. "Have you ever seen a concentrated animal feeding operation, Beth?" When she shook her head, he said, "I have. I worked one summer at a pig company. It was brutal. Those animals are mistreated from the moment they're born until they're finally put outta their misery—and half the time, that's done half-assed too, so they suffer 'til the very end." He took a big bite of his stew, as though for emphasis. "I'd rather know the animal I'm eating lived the life it was supposed to and was killed humanely. I don't let them suffer."

She hated to concede, but he had a point, and a way of making her look at it that she hadn't considered before. "Okay, but what about the sport hunters you guide?"

He lifted a shoulder. "Some of them take the meat, and some don't, but I don't let none of it go to waste. If the hunters only want their trophies, they take whatever token they think is important, and I keep the rest. Sometimes I eat it, and sometimes it goes to folks that need it more. I usually end up dropping off a couple hundred pounds of meat in Endline for the town folks when I go twice a year to replenish supplies."

"Oh." She didn't look up at him again as she took another tentative bite of the meat. "What about if you have a hunter who just injures the animal?"

He sighed. "That's happened a few times. Usually, it's some pansy-assed stockbroker, or somethin', who couldn't keep up with me for miles, so I end up tracking the animal and finishing it off. If it's not too bad, I try to save it and let it go back to its life. And I never accept those incompetent assholes as clients again."

"Oh," she said again, nodding. "That's very decent of you."

He rolled his eyes, as though she had insulted him instead of complimented him. "Thanks, girl."

"I'm not a girl," she said again, more firmly.

With an ambiguous look, he turned his attention back to his bowl. "I know that," he mumbled, saying nothing else throughout the meal.

Of course she wasn't a girl. Stripped of that parka and wearing those tight jeans—were they called skinny jeans?—and a snug sweater in that same sort of some material as her hat, there was no mistaking her for a girl. She had nicely rounded breasts, long legs for her frame that seemed built to wrap around a man's waist, and curvy hips that could take the pressure of a man's hands holding them while he pounded into her.

Fuck, she was definitely not a girl. He stirred the fire with the poker as he listened to her sing softly while she put away the dishes she had insisted on washing. He'd half-expected to have to redo them himself, but after watching her for a couple of minutes, he'd realized she could handle the task. It might be the first time she'd ever done them, but washing dishes wasn't exactly brain surgery.

Not that he'd count her out of that profession, or any other. She was obviously well educated and came from money. Smart and sassy, only a fool would underestimate her prospects.

Only a goddamn fool would be imagining what it might be like to taste the honeyed skin of her neck, or cup her ass in his hands, knowing the kind of man he was. He'd left most of his past behind when he'd come to Alaska eight years ago, but he was smart enough to know a woman like that was out of his league. Never mind the fifteen years separating them. His past and her future would never mesh, so fantasizing about touching that luscious woman was plain foolishness.

When her daddy and crew arrived tomorrow, he'd have to be damned sure he hid any hint of attraction he felt. The Wyndam group was paying enough for him to be able to take a season off and have some personal space again. After a few months of people, he always got fed up and had to have a breather. He couldn't risk alienating such clients, and hitting on the teenage daughter, even if she was technically legal, was a surefire way to do so.

What was wrong with him anyway, that he was feeling lustful for a teenager? Dammit, he should have stopped by the whorehouse the last time he was in Endline. In a region where men were far more common than women, it was about the only sure thing a man could find in these parts. Most women were already partnered up with someone, and since he wasn't the partnering-up type, whores were a viable option. The last couple of trips though, he'd passed on by the nondescript house on the edge of the city, finding the idea of meaningless sex that he paid for was no more satisfying or appealing than his own hand.

Now, he wished he'd dipped his dick in all six of the whores working there, with the appropriate raingear, of course. Apparently, his body was feeling the itch for feminine companionship, and if he'd scratched it three months ago, he wouldn't be stifling back a groan at the sight of that sweetly rounded ass in those tight jeans as she bent over to put the stewpot into the drawer under the oven.

She joined him all too quickly, and he was equal parts disappointed and relieved when she sat down on the same couch as him, instead of heading on to her room. At least she left a cushion between them. Damn, didn't the girl have any common sense? She was alone with a man she didn't know, and he could take advantage of her without her consent, if he was a different sort. Hell, didn't her daddy have any common sense? Who sent their teenage daughter to a strange man's home alone? Without thought, he voiced his opinion. "What kind of stupid is your father that he just lets you travel alone and sends you wherever without a proper escort?"

She cocked her head, looking both amused and angry. "He didn't let me travel anywhere. I'm an adult, and I booked my ticket. I'd planned to stay in Fairbanks and just meet up with him for a few days in Edgeline."

"Endline," he interrupted.

She waved a hand. "Yeah, whatever. Except I didn't realize the distance, or the difficulty with traveling. I thought I'd surprise him, but it ended up being an inconvenience." Beth shrugged. "Same as always, I guess."

"Still, his solution was to send his little girl on ahead to stay alone with a strange man?" He shook his head. "Ain't no way in hell my daughter would do such a foolish thing. I could be all kinds of pervert, girl."

She did grin then. "Really? What kinds are you?"

That wasn't the response he'd expected, and he was disconcerted to have his cheeks warming. "That's not the point. I'm just surprised by how lax y'all are with safety."

Beth's lips twitched. "I guess Daddy figured you'd be a professional, since you have a bazillion good references from previous guests." She shrugged. "Or maybe he didn't think at all. I'm not high on his list of priorities."

His frown deepened. "Then he needs to reorder his priorities." At her careless shrug, his irritation softened, and he warred with the urge to pick up her hand and offer comfort. Only the knowledge that innocent comfort could lead to carnal actions kept his hand firmly on his own leg. "What about you? Don't you have more regard for your safety?"

"I can take care of myself."

She spoke with such conviction that he couldn't help scoffing, though it probably insulted her. "Look, girl—"

"Beth," she put in.

"Beth," he repeated with gritted teeth. "You couldn't take on a wet kitten and win."

She cocked a brow. "Challenge accepted."

"Huh?" He frowned. "I don't actually have a wet kitten, you know," he said drily after a moment.

Beth's obstinate expression hardened further. "Get up."

"What?"

She got to her feet, moving lightly. "Come on. Get off your ass and come at me, Mr. All Kinds of Perv."

Feeling amused, and a tad indulgent, he stood up. He wasn't going to hurt her none, but a little lesson wouldn't be a bad idea. Ms. Wyndam needed to know she wasn't as tough as she thought, before she was actually in a situation that led her to act with foolish overconfidence. "All right, little girl. I'm gonna school you."

She didn't reply, just poising on the balls of her feet as she waited for him to make a move. Something about her stance annoyed him, and he found himself taking it more seriously than he'd intended. His first plan had been a direct assault, but he found himself drawing on the training he'd learned in the Army. He came at her to the right, before switching to the left at the last minute.

He'd expected to end up with her struggling in his arms, so the knee she rammed into his stomach was a shock. Reed let out a harsh breath and dropped to his knees from a combination of pain and surprise. In two seconds, that little hellcat kicked his shoulder, sending him reeling backward. She landed on his chest with enough force to make him exhale loudly, and her fingers hesitated within millimeters of his eyes. "Now, this is the point where I'd blind you, or rip your balls off..." She patted his thigh just an inch below his package. "If you were really trying to hurt me."

With a sunny smile, she bounded off him, offering him a hand up that he disdained. She shrugged and returned to the couch. "Poor loser."

He wasn't seriously injured, aside from his pride, and he was on his feet quickly, glaring down at her as he rubbed the sore spot on his shoulder. "How'd you learn all that?"

She smiled breezily. "I was into those martial arts movies for a while, so my mom got me private lessons. I know a couple of formal types of martial arts, but my instructor also taught me some dirty tricks."

"I'll say." He was reluctantly impressed as he sat down in his former spot.

"So, *kitten*," she asked sweetly, "Do you think I can take care of myself?"

"I sure hope so. After that kung fu shit, I'm relying on you to take care of me too, if bad guys come."

"No bad guys here," she said with a grin.

With more seriousness than he'd intended, he said, "Don't be too sure, Beth."

She regarded him for a moment, as though peering deep into his soul. "No bad guys here," she said again, and then lightened the mood by patting his thigh. "But I'll protect you if they show up."

He laughed with her, all the while conscious of her hand on his leg, and the way her breasts strained against the soft sweater as she leaned across the gap separating them to be able to touch him. His amusement fled as he contemplated grabbing a handful of the hair she'd brushed into a shining curtain of silvery blonde and bridging the distance. She couldn't weigh more than a hundred pounds, and he didn't think she'd resist if he lifted her to sit on his lap. It had been a while since a woman had desired him for any reason besides being paid to, but he was pretty sure he remembered that smoky look that came to her eyes, or the way an aroused woman licked her pouty lips.

If Beth wanted him, he was in big trouble. Her father couldn't arrive soon enough to save him from making a mistake that he seemed helpless to stop. Getting through the evening without touching her was an exercise in will power, and he was relieved when she started yawning around nine and made her way to bed. Thank goodness the rest of the group was coming tomorrow. His tenuous self-control needed reinforcements.

Chapter Two

BETH HAD SLEPT WELL last night, despite her lack of progress in getting Reed into bed. In retrospect, she'd figured out he wasn't the kind of man who would take a young woman to bed for a one-night stand—especially if he discovered she was still a member of the V-club. He seemed like the torn-up, angst-ridden type, who wouldn't allow himself to easily give in to desire for someone he thought he shouldn't want. In the light of day—though that was more a habitual phrase than a reality, with the grayish light coming through the windows—she was still optimistic. Yeah, her dad would put a crimp in her attempts, but there would be two weeks to wear down his resistance. She didn't think she'd been wrong about the spark of interest in his blue eyes last night, and she sure hadn't been imagining the erection he'd had, even in the midst of their mock sparring.

He looked dour when she joined him at the table. "You're up early," he said, making it an accusation.

She smiled. "I'm a morning person, Reed."

"I'm not." He glared at his oatmeal. "Even worse without coffee."

"Do you want me to make some?"

He frowned. "I can make my own damned coffee, but the pot's broken."

She put up a hand. "Easy there. I'm not Snow White." He just blinked, clearly confused. She giggled. "As in the seven dwarves, which included Grumpy?" His confusion cleared, but he didn't look amused. For some reason, his surliness made her want to snicker instead of respond in kind today, and she chuckled.

"Laugh it up, but I got bad news." He gestured to some expensive-looking communication equipment on a nearby table. "Your old man radioed. There's bad weather there, heading our way, and they won't be coming today."

"Oh?" She could barely hide her excitement. "Tomorrow then?"

He snorted. "More like four or five days. Three, if we're lucky."

"Oh, then I hope I get lucky." She said it casually, but had to bite back a grin at her hidden meaning. Her chances of doing so had just risen astronomically.

"You'll have to find some way to entertain yourself," he said as he pushed the serving bowl of oatmeal her way before scooping up his own now-empty bowl to take to the sink. "With bad weather coming, I need to take stock of everything. Make sure we have enough provisions, like firewood." His large hands made quick work of washing the bowl. "First thing I gotta do is check the gennies." He turned from the sink. "Generators."

Beth resisted the urge to roll her eyes, but exasperation still stained her voice. "Yeah, I know what a genny is, Reed."

He nodded. "There's probably not much you don't know."

Delivered in that tone, it was difficult to tell if he was making conversation, paying a compliment, or casting aspersions. She tilted her head sideways, making her hair fall over her shoulder and down the front of the sleep tank she wore. "Why do you say that?"

He lifted a shoulder. "Rich folks, clearly a good education. I'm guessin' some prestigious private school? You're probably going to the best university money can buy."

It was definitely starting to sound like a negative, and her back tensed. "I went to a private school, but not the elite boarding school my dad wanted. Fortunately, my mom likes having me around." She smiled a bit, hoping to coax one from him. "As far as school goes, I haven't actually enrolled yet. I'm taking a year off between high school and college."

He snorted. "Who wouldn't love to do that? 'Course, most of us don't have rich parents to pay for such an indulgence."

The nasty tone underlying his words made her frown. "Is it a crime to be rich?"

"If it is, I sure want to be a criminal," he said with a twist of his lips. "Ain't no crime to enjoy your daddy's money, but it'd be nice if you appreciate it too and acknowledge you're luckier than most."

"My mother's actually," she said softly. At his blank look, she added, "It's my mother's money that Daddy wastes so extravagantly. She's from a family of Texas oil barons so embarrassingly wealthy that his ridiculous frivolities aren't even a blip on her radar." She lowered her voice. "Is that what you wanted to hear, Reed? I'm just some spoiled little rich girl, out for a good time?"

One side of his mouth raised, and he seemed to be poised to say something. Finally, with an air that suggested he'd changed his mind, he just said, "You ain't a girl, remember?" Without waiting for a reply, he turned and left the kitchen, calling over his shoulder, "There's some books on the shelf in the great room. Movies and such too, but no cable or TV stations. You might have to see to your own lunch, dependin' on how long the genny and other preps take me."

Beth watched him go, her brain whirring. Obviously, the man had a hang-up on wealth. Apparently, not only did she have to get him to see her as a fully grown woman, but she also had to tackle his prejudice toward privilege. Toying with the spoon in her oatmeal, she wondered if it was worth it. There were other men out there. Men far easier to control. Even if she didn't have her parents' bank account as an enticement, she knew her own petite curves and striking blonde hair gave her a natural advantage when it came to conquering men. She'd never been one to rely on such wiles before, but it wouldn't take much to tempt one of the men of her acquaintance into helping her dispense with the V-card. Not that she really cared about doing so. Virginity was neither something she prized nor baggage she couldn't wait to shed. She'd always assumed she would know when it was the right guy and the right time.

Every instinct inside her was clamoring for Reed, telling her it was the right time and the right guy. He was going to make it difficult, but she decided she wasn't ready to give up on her campaign just yet.

If she wanted something badly enough, she could almost always make it happen—often without the wealth he disparaged so obviously—and she wanted Reed very much. Despite their short acquaintance, and her only superficial knowledge of all other aspects of the man, she was convinced he was meant to be hers. It sounded silly, even to her, and she was glad she didn't have to explain to anyone how she knew on an instinctual level that he was the man she'd been waiting for to bring her body fully to life.

Reed came in around two for a late lunch. He wasn't finished with the generator yet, having decided it needed a complete tune-up, and he hadn't even started chopping firewood, but his stomach was growling like a bear. As he stripped off his coat, a tantalizing aroma hit his nose, and his stomach growled harder. With an impatient kick of his boots toward the door, he walked farther into the house, pausing in the kitchen.

Inhaling deeply, he detected garlic and roasting meat. With an appreciative hum, he opened the oven door a bit to peek in. The sight of a bison roast neatly surrounded by chopped potatoes, carrots, and leeks made his stomach gurgle.

"It's not ready yet."

He straightened abruptly at the sound of her voice behind him. Whatever he'd planned to say was lost at the sight of her in a skimpy white robe that left little to the imagination. Reed couldn't keep his eyes from dipping momentarily to her breasts, where the faintest pink from her areolas showed through the thin silk, but immediately brought his eyes upward, to lodge on her ponytail.

She put her arms around her torso. "I was just coming to baste it once more before I got in the shower."

He nodded. "I can handle that." Amazingly, his voice still worked, though it sounded raspy.

She smiled. "Thanks. I'll hit the shower then."

Reed nodded again, watching her turn around and walk back toward the guest quarters. He couldn't tear his gaze from her sweet little ass caressed by the silk. His cock hardened at the thought of her naked underneath it, and he briefly considered putting the table to a new use, for which it had never been intended.

With a sigh that was part regret and part self-loathing for the inappropriate attraction, he turned back to the oven and quickly basted the meal she had put together. After that, he slapped together a peanut butter and jam sandwich, practically swallowing it whole in his efforts to get back outside. The farther he was from her, the better for his self-control.

After a quick glass of milk, he washed up and started to put his boots on again. He hesitated, realizing he hadn't thought to ask her when the roast would be finished. After she'd gone to so much trouble, he didn't want to be late. After another second's hesitation, he left his boots by the door and walked over to the entrance to the guestrooms. He couldn't hear the shower running, so he assumed she was finished. At the bathroom, he lifted his hand to tap on the door, but hesitated when he heard a splash.

Reed barely bit back a groan as his mind insisted on supplying him with an image of the object of his desires squeezed into that tiny tub. As he imagined her fingers working over her skin, spreading bubbles—because she had to be the bubble bath type—a moan filled the air. For a second, he thought it had escaped him, and he bit hard on his tongue. It was only when it came again, along with the sound of sloshing water in a rhythmic fashion, that he realized Beth had made the soft moan. Instantly, he knew what she was doing, and again, his mind projected an image. The only practical way she could touch herself in that tub was to hang one leg over the side, to fully open her thighs.

Her hand would have enough room to slip between at that point, to touch and tease the wet heat between her legs. She moaned again, and he bit harder on his tongue as his dick strained against his jeans. No doubt, she was stroking her clit with those long fingers of hers.

Reed knew he should walk away, but the sounds of her self-pleasure kept him glued to the spot long past when the decent thing would have been to give her privacy. His cock pulsed in time with her panted breaths and low groans of satisfaction. He gripped the doorjamb when she cried out quietly and was grateful for its support when she uttered a single word.

"Reed," she whispered in a soft, breathy murmur that sounded like ecstasy given voice.

He clutched the wood until his knuckles turned white before he was able to regain control and walk away from the bathroom as quietly as possible. He reentered his living area and put on his outdoor gear quickly, almost running to the shed housing the generator in an attempt to flee the natural male impulse that was urging him to turn around, go back into the house, and find Beth, so he could finish what she'd started.

He cursed a blue streak in the shed as he tried to return his attention to the generator. Temptation personified was in his house, and he was out in the cold, literally. Life really sucked sometimes. Here was something he wanted desperately, but circumstances made it impossible. "Story of my life," he said aloud as he grasped the wrench. It was going to be a long three days until the rest of the party arrived. He hoped the weather improved quickly.

Chapter Three

BETH HAD SPENT THE afternoon cleaning and straightening the already tidy great room and kitchen after putting on the roast. It had seemed like a productive use of her time, and perhaps she'd hoped to impress him with her Suzy Homemaker skills. Not that it seemed likely to work. The man could kill his own dinner, cook it, and clean up after himself. What did he need a woman around for?

Well, besides the obvious. Her pussy tingled as she recalled the fantasy she'd had in the bathtub, imagining Reed's hand bringing her to orgasm. Foolish optimism soared, and she found herself fervently hoping they would remain snowbound for weeks, without interruption. Surely, in that time, she could gain his attention.

She had just taken out the roast when he opened the door. With a smile in his direction, she said, "Perfect timing. I just need to make some jus, and we're ready to eat."

He looked cold and haggard. "I'll have a quick wash." Something about his eyes and tone made the words sound more suggestive than they should have, making her mind jump back to her self-pleasuring session in the bathroom earlier in the day. Was he planning to do the same?

Keeping her attention on the skillet was difficult as she imagined him stripping off all his clothes and stepping into his shower. She didn't know if was similar to the one in his guest quarters, but her mind conjured up that tiny stall, trying to figure out the logistics of two bodies squeezed in there together.

He came back to the table ten minutes later, wearing faded jeans that hugged like a second skin and a thick tweed sweater. She'd already set the table and now put out the food. "I don't know where you keep your wine, but a nice red would pair well with this."

He frowned. "You're eighteen."

She nodded.

"That's not old enough to drink."

Beth laughed. "My mom comes from French stock, so wine is practically water in her view. She probably slipped it into my sippy cups as a child." At his look, she put up a hand. "I'm kidding. I remember having my first sip at age six, on Thanksgiving. It was only recently that I've been promoted to having a full glass with some meals."

He still looked disapproving. "I don't have any wine."

"Oh." She tilted her head. "Are you out, or...?"

"I don't drink it, and I don't buy it," he said with an air of finality. "Guests can bring their own, but I don't provide it."

There was more to that, but she decided not to pry for the moment as she got them glasses of water instead. She sat across from him and put the linen napkin over her lap. She'd found the set of table linens in a bottom drawer, and though they'd been a bit dusty, a quick shakeout had made them usable.

"This is real nice." He passed her the serving platter first before loading his plate. "You didn't have to do this, Beth."

She shrugged. "I know, but I didn't have much else going on. I'm sure you don't feel like cooking or waiting on me after a day spent out in that weather." With a reflexive look out the nearest window, she shivered.

"Still, ain't your job." He took a mouthful of the meat, eyes closing for a moment as though he savored it. "It's my job, in point of fact."

Beth grinned. "As I said, I wasn't doing anything else. I enjoyed it."

"Where'd you learn to cook?"

Her grin widened. "I wouldn't call my skills cooking, exactly. I took a culinary unit in school, and I sometimes hang out in the kitchen at home, watching the chef. I can cover the basics, but that's about it."

He lifted a forkful of meat and carrots. "This ain't the basics, girl." With an appreciative sound, he ate another bite.

She blushed. "Well, thanks. I'm glad it wasn't a disaster."

"No disaster here. This is like a restaurant meal, which is pretty uncommon around here."

Again, she looked outside. "It's so dark and isolated. Do you ever get restless?"

He paused to sip his water, looking thoughtful. "I suppose, but if I do, I go for a walk or take out the snowmobile."

"I meant being so alone out here, and not being near other people or things to do." Licking her lips, she asked, "Don't you get lonely?"

He shook his head. "No. By the time I'm done with guests for the year, I'm usually heartily sick of people."

"The silence doesn't get to you, out here on your own?"

Reed shook his head. "Nah, my own company don't bother me. It's other people I usually can't stand."

She smiled, though she didn't think he was entirely joking. "I think I would miss being able to walk down the street for coffee or Thai food."

He nodded. "This life ain't for most, Beth."

Taking a deep breath for courage, she said, "Plus, I'd get lonely. I couldn't live out here alone, with no one to talk to." He didn't answer, so she prodded a bit more. "I mean, how do you ever date around here?"

Reed looked up from his plate. "I don't."

She cleared her throat. "Well, how are you ever going to meet someone to spend your life with?"

"Don't want to." He seemed far more interested in the food than the conversation.

Feeling a tad exasperated by his lack of communication, she said, "Fine, but what about sex? Don't you miss that?"

He froze before carefully lowering his fork. "Tomorrow's goin' to be a busy day again, so I can finish the rest of the chores before the bad weather really hits. I spent most of the day fooling with the main and backup generators, so you'll have to entertain yourself again."

She frowned. "Are you just going to ignore my question?"

"Damn right I am. It's personal and not appropriate."

With a sigh of frustration, she returned to her meal, her mind still buzzing with curiosity. Surely, he had sex sometimes, but she couldn't puzzle out how. Unless... "Have you ever slept with any of the women who hire you?"

He sighed, long and loud. "They've all been wives or girlfriends of my clients, Beth."

She arched a brow. "But do you?"

Reed looked offended. "'Course I don't. Belonging to someone else is a stop sign for me, girl, as it should be for anyone."

Beth smiled. "I agree, though my parents have a very different sort of viewpoint."

He curled his lip. "Ain't a real marriage if you can't be true to each other."

She swallowed the lump of moisture his words had brought to her throat. "Again, I agree."

He returned his attention to his dinner, and they finished soon after. "That was real good," he praised again. "I'm lookin' forward to the leftovers already."

She glowed with pride. "Thanks. I didn't make any dessert. I'm not much of a baker, and you didn't have any way to cheat."

He arched a brow. "What'd you mean?"

"Oh, brownie mix or something. All you had was the raw materials, but I don't know how to make them into something edible."

He patted her shoulder. "All you can do is try. If it don't turn out how you wanted, you just try again."

It was good advice, and she seized the moment as he leaned down to retrieve his plate. Beth stretched on her toes and pressed a kiss to his cheek. He froze, but didn't move away. Emboldened, she stepped a bit closer, running her lips along his jaw line, but not trying to kiss him. "Maybe you could teach me," she said softly, near his mouth.

He still stood stiffly. "Teach you what, girl?"

"Lots of things," she said in what she hoped was a seductive purr. "Like how to make brownies."

After a moment, his jaw unclenched, and he stepped away from her, clearly planning to ignore her physical overtures. "I don't have time to teach you nothing, Beth." Without another glance at her, he turned toward the sink and began to wash the dishes, giving the task all his attention.

With a sigh, Beth scraped her plate and added it to the sink, before she put away the leftovers. Reed Nixon was proving to be a difficult nut to crack. She wasn't surprised when he left the kitchen a few minutes later and went down the hall to his private living space, instead of the great room. Apparently, there would be no repeat of last night.

Feeling a bit defeated, she went to the great room to peruse his selection of movies. Reading was a favorite activity, but she didn't have the necessary focus to concentrate tonight. A movie wouldn't require as much attention. In no time, she settled on "30 Days of Night," deciding it was appropriate based on the description. It was engrossing, but disgusting, and she was burying her face in a pillow at a particularly gruesome scene about an hour in when the couch dipped. Peeking out of her pillow, she saw Reed sit down on the cushion he'd used last night.

"Don't be a sissy, girl." He tugged the pillow from her and put it on the cushion between them. "Ain't real, you know."

Beth rolled her eyes. "Of course it isn't, but it's still gross."

He lifted a shoulder. "I suppose, but reality is worse." A frown followed his words, as though he regretted speaking so freely.

Cautiously, she asked, "You've seen worse in real life?"

After a quick hesitation, he nodded. "I was in the Army. Lost my squad in Kandahar."

"I'm sorry." What could she say besides that, never having experienced anything even close to comparable?

He nodded, his attention seemingly remaining on the screen, though his eyes looked haunted.

"Doesn't this movie creep you out, living out here, especially during the darker side of the year?" Beth shivered. "They aren't even the sexy vampires."

Reed looked at her, arching a brow. "Sexy vampires? When the hell did vampires become sexy?"

She frowned. "I don't know."

He rolled his eyes. "Well, what makes a vampire sexy?"

She chewed on her lower lip, considering her answer. "Honestly, I'm not a big horror fan, but I've seen some movies and read some books. I guess the vamps that struggle with retaining their humanity. Or the ones who are so seductive that it doesn't matter if they do bad things. Dracula was like that, at least in that old movie with Keanu Reeves."

Reed snorted. "'Old movie.' Damn, that definition has changed. I don't think the movie version of Dracula was much like the one in the book, least not the book I read."

"Some people consider the sparkling ones sexy." At his look of incomprehension, she said, "There's a set of books for young adults with vampires who sparkle in the sun, instead of burning up. Some of the vamps don't feed on humans. One of those falls for a dorky high school girl and turns stalking into an art form. He even watches her sleep...in her room...when she doesn't know he's there."

Reed blew out a low breath. "That's the kinda shit that passes for romantic among young girls these days?" He snorted again. "Glad I'm old then."

She shrugged. "I didn't say that was romantic. His undying love is sweet, and that's what attracts most of the readers, but the ways he expresses it...classic stalker."

Gesturing toward the screen, where Josh Hartnett was currently frying the bad female vampire with ultraviolet light, he said, "Gimme those types of vampires any day."

She cast a glance out the window, finding it was fully dark and not the twilight-like light they got during midday. "Not right now, please."

Reed chuckled. "What's the matter? You'll just kung fu their asses."

She looked away from the screen again as more blood spattered. "I definitely picked the wrong movie. I'm going to have nightmares tonight." It was the perfect moment for him to offer to check on her, or for her to ask to let her sleep with him, but neither spoke a word. She imagined it hadn't even occurred to Reed, and she wasn't ready for another round of humiliation after his rejection at dinner.

"Watch some fluffy bunny crap before you go to sleep. You'll be fine." He yawned and stretched. "Speaking of, I'm headin' to bed. It's another long day tomorrow." Reed stood up and wandered back to his side of the house.

Beth watched him go, wondering why he'd even bothered to come out for a few minutes. She wished she knew what he was thinking.

What had he been thinking? He'd been secure from temptation in his room, reading a book, when he'd abruptly decided to check on her. Just as a courtesy. Bullshit. Reed squirmed, thinking to himself that he'd gone back out there with the full intention of giving that girl some lessons, and not in how to make brownies. If she hadn't been sitting on the couch, face pressed into a pillow like a scared kid, he would have followed through. Instead, that pose had reminded him of her tender years, and he'd been unable to carry out his intentions. It didn't matter if she was legal when she was clearly inexperienced.

Or maybe she wasn't. He ran a hair through his overgrown locks, frustration eating at him. She'd seemed pretty brave and confident with her come-on after dinner, going so far as the kiss him. It was hardly a kiss, but still took a dose of courage. Or security with one's own sexuality. Was he in here tearing himself to shreds with indecision, having wrongly guessed she was still fairly innocent, though probably not a virgin? Was she an experienced seductress, and he was denying himself needlessly?

Feeling torn and confused, Reed tore open the door to his room and strode back to the great room, intent on at least having a discussion about the simmering attraction. Instead, he found the TV and lights off, and the couch unoccupied. While he'd been struggling with his demons, she'd gone on to bed. No doubt, she was in there sleeping like a baby right now.

Or touching herself. His cock twitched at the thought. Indecision kept him glued to the spot for a moment, before he gave up and headed back to his room. Her early bedtime had saved him from making a mistake. There couldn't be anything between them. His brain knew it, and his dick just had to accept it.

Chapter Four

THERE WAS A THICK BLANKET of new snow on the ground when Beth woke the next morning. She'd slept in a bit, having tossed and turned last night, her body burning for the kind of relief only Reed could provide. Her hand was a pale substitute for what she really craved, and two self-induced orgasms had done nothing to chill her heated body. Eventually, she'd fallen asleep, though she vaguely remembered dreaming of vampires and sex, though she didn't think they were the sexy vampires. The dreams had been disquieting, not satisfying.

A hot shower had restored her equilibrium, and she was feeling herself again when she entered the kitchen, hoping to find Reed. It was later than yesterday, and she must have already missed him. A lone plate in the dish drainer and a cast iron skillet that appeared to have been dried on the burner after washing were the only things he'd left behind to indicate he'd already come and gone.

He hadn't even left a note, she thought sourly, as she rummaged through his cabinets until she found some cereal. The milk was in a glass mason jar, and she took a cautious sniff. It smelled okay, so she poured some on her cereal. The first taste made her grimace, and she guessed it was powdered milk. "Yuck." Only determination not to waste food got her through the bowl of ickiness. "No more cold cereal in the mornings," she said aloud, as she tidied behind herself.

Wanting to feel useful, Beth once again took stock of the food items, including the walk-in pantry and large freezer in the room adjacent the kitchen. His small selection of cookbooks came in handy, particularly when she needed a substitute for white wine. After planning the dinner menu, she still had several hours before she'd actually need to cook it. There were still leftovers from their previous meals for lunch, so what else could she do?

Even though she as technically a paying customer, it seemed wrong to be sitting around comfortably in his house while he was out in the cold, working to make sure they were comfortable during the approaching storm. Biting her lip, Beth decided to see if she could find him. The parka and boots were cumbersome, but she knew they would provide welcome warmth as soon as she left the cozy cabin.

She made slow progress out the front door and around the small house. It was larger on the inside than it appeared from the outside, but she knew that was because the designer—Reed?—had made the cabin longer rather than wider. She scanned the collection of outbuildings and the surrounding area, finding no easily detectable sign of Reed. The air was so cold her sigh was visible as she trekked through the deep snow toward the nearest shed.

She opened the door timidly, not certain what to expect. Reed wasn't there, but a huge collection of firewood was stacked up to the ceiling all around the perimeter. There was a small workspace in the middle, with a solid section of trunk and a gleaming ax buried in it. Recalling that he planned to chop firewood today, she walked over to the ax and block, examining it critically.

While she had never cut wood, she had seen enough movies to figure out the large diameters of the chunks of wood would have to be split into smaller sections. Quarters, probably, she guessed upon conjuring a mental picture of the wood stacked in the holder near the fireplace in the great room.

How hard could it be? Physically, it was surely taxing, but if she could handle that aspect, it would be a straightforward task. Beth didn't try to convince herself that she would be nearly as useful at the job as Reed, but even if she only managed a little bit, she'd be saving him some work.

She put one foot on the block and grasped the ax with both hands, pulling firmly to remove it from its resting place. To her pleasant surprise, the implement slid out smoothly, and she was soon holding it in her hands. She frowned at the head of the ax, wondering why one side was flat. It didn't look like the axes she'd seen behind glass doors in the stairwells at her mother's high-rise apartment in Manhattan. The dual-sided head probably served two functions, but she had no idea what to do with the flat one. Hopefully, the sharp side would be enough.

The next task was the lift one of the pieces of log onto the chopping block. She set down the ax carefully and bent to the nearest stack. It took some careful finagling, but she managed to work loose a piece from the bottom of the heap, being much too short to try to grab from the top. It was heavy, but more awkward than anything. Persistence paid off, and she soon had it positioned on the block.

Mimicking what she'd seen in movies, Beth stood with her feet spaced widely apart and lifted the ax straight over her head. After a couple of practice strikes, to make sure she was bringing it down smoothly and in a straight line, she gave a solid whack with the tool. A girlish squeal of delight escaped her when the ax head penetrated the center of the log. Two more chops, and the piece of wood split in two. With a victorious grin, she moved one section aside to split the other into fourths before repeating with the remaining piece.

It was slow and tedious work, and she was soon hot and sweaty, though she wouldn't have believed it would be possible with the temperature outside. She paused for a moment to strip off her coat and lay it across the pile before resuming her task.

Within an hour, her arms and shoulders ached, but she had a nice little pile of wood nearby. It was certainly enough to fill the box in the great room, and maybe half-fill the box by the old pot-bellied stove in the bunkroom. Not that they probably needed to worry about that. In fact, if it got too cold, they might have to confine themselves to one room to conserve fuel. She wondered if he had a fireplace in his room, and if he would invite her to share it.

Lost in her sweet little daydream of Reed taking her to his bed and making love to her by the glow of a fire, it took her a moment to realize he was calling her name, and not in her fantasy. Blinking, she looked away from the log to find an angry-looking Reed standing in the doorway. "What?"

"I said, what the hell you doin', girl?" He looked disgusted as he strode across the shed, skirting her meager pile of split wood, to wrench the ax from her hand. "Are you crazy? You don't use a maul without safety goggles, work gloves, and a lick of common sense."

"Oh." She stared at the tool that seemed to have worn permanent grooves in her palms during the last hour. *Maul.* "I thought it was an ax." He cursed something that would have shocked her grandmother, but she'd heard worse from the girls in her private school. Beth folded her arms and stared at him. "What's your problem?"

"My problem?" He shook the maul at her. "My problem is, my insurance don't cover fools doing stupid things to themselves." With obvious disgust, he tossed the maul behind him. "What possessed you?"

She was torn between the urge to cry and the urge to smack him. Beth decided on neither. With a sniff, she said, "I was trying to help you."

"How's it goin' to help me if you get yourself killed, woman?"

A grin blossomed without her permission. "Finally, I'm no longer 'girl.'"

He cursed again. "This ain't a joke, Beth."

"I know that." She went for a soft tone to placate him. "You're overreacting though. I was doing an okay job." Pointing to the neat stacks beside her, she said, "I'm sure I'm nowhere as fast as you, but I made some headway."

He glowered at the pile, and then kicked it with the sturdy snow boot on his left food. She gasped as the pieces went everywhere, feeling more outraged that he'd disrupted her pile than that he'd yelled at her. Until that display of temper, she'd thought he had acted out of concern, not anger. "You're just a bully." Bending over, she started gathering the wood into her arms, intent on delivering it safely to the house, since she'd started the job. He could damn well finish the rest though. It'd serve him right if the entire woodpile toppled over onto him.

Doing a fair bit of cursing herself, she elbowed him out of her way to get a stick behind him. At the same time, he reached for her arm. "Let go of me, you jackass." With a violent tug, she pulled free. The quick motion upset her center of gravity in the unwieldy boots, and she flailed her arms, cursing again as the wood flew everywhere.

Beth fell forward hard, barely catching herself on her hands to prevent her face from smacking into the ground as her torso had done. "Look what you did," she snarled, tears coming to her eyes. "Now I have to pick all that up again."

Anger fueled her, and she got quickly to her feet, stomping to the nearest piece. Wielding it like a pointer, she whirled around to him, shaking it in his direction. "You don't have to be so mean or rude. I was trying to help. Some people would just say thank you."

"Beth." He held out a hand, his face turning pale.

Concern chased away a bit of her anger, and she lowered her stick. "What's wrong? You look terrible."

His expression tightened, but his complexion remained on the gray side. "Honey, look down."

The endearment caught her by surprise, but wasn't nearly as surprising as the red splotch spreading across her lavender sweater. "What the hell?" For a moment, her brain couldn't identify the substance. "Blood?" As soon as she realized she was bleeding, the pain suddenly hit. She dropped the wood and put her hand over the wound. "Ouch." Though she was still angry with him, Beth didn't reject his help when he put an arm around her waist and led her back to the cabin.

Halfway there, she started to feel a little faint, though probably from shock instead of blood loss, she decided critically. As she wobbled, Reed bent down and swept her into his arms, striding through the snow with the same ease she would have walking down a New York City sidewalk. He shouldered open the door and took her straight to the table, sitting her on top of the smooth surface.

"Don't move," he admonished before turning from her to go to the sink, stripping off his heavy coat in the process. When he returned, he held a large white box with a red cross on it. It was definitely more elaborate than the typical first-aid kit. He looked a bit nonplussed when he asked, "Can you take off your sweater?"

This was certainly not the scenario she had imagined would lead to her getting undressed in front of him. Still feeling a bit shaky, she eased off the sweater, leaving her in just the satin camisole she wore underneath. Despite the pain from her cut, she shivered when his fingers gently lowered the left strap and pulled down the top a bit, so he could get a better look.

"Sorry," he said.

She shook her head, not wanting to explain the cause of her indrawn breath. "How bad is it?"

"Gimme a sec." He opened a crinkly pouch of saline solution and poured it over the wound. She winced a bit, but didn't find it too uncomfortable. "I think some butterfly Band-Aids will fix you right up, girl. Looks like you fell on the edge of the ax. Ain't gonna need stitches."

"Thank goodness." She tilted her head. "Can you do that, I mean, if I'd needed it?"

Reed nodded, though his gaze remained focused on her wound as he dabbed it gently with sterile gauze. "Had some medical training in the Army." Setting aside the gauze, he reached for a box of bandages.

"Got some painkillers and everything, but I ain't never needed to perform surgery on any of my clients." Looking away briefly from her flesh, he glowered at her. "Ain't never had one dumb enough to go out lookin' for this kind of trouble."

She returned his glare. "I promise I won't help you again, you brusque bastard. I'll just sit on my ass and eat bonbons all day until Daddy arrives."

He snorted. "You already lost the argument when you got to resort to name-calling." Reed opened the first bandage. "Besides, ain't got no bonbons, Beth."

For some reason, that struck her as funny, and she started giggling. Trying to stifle the response with her hand did no good, and she ended up laughing. To her surprise, he joined in with a small chuckle.

"Now, hold still. I gotta get the edges back together."

It struck her that he was awfully close to her left breast as he gently pulled the wound taut and applied the first bandage. It was a strange mix of pain and pleasure that assaulted her for the next five minutes, as he affixed three more bandages before covering it all with a large adhesive pad. The tugging and pulling of the wound hurt, but his fingers on her skin were heaven.

"There. That should fix ya' up. You'll need to keep it as clean as possible, and we should check it again tomorrow." His fingers slid under the strap of her white cami to slide it back up her arm. "Just let me know if it starts hurtin' real bad or something though."

She nodded, compelled to put her hand over his, leaving the strap partially on her shoulder. "Thanks, Reed."

He nodded, and his cheeks bloomed with color. She didn't know if it was embarrassment or a reaction to her touch, and his words didn't help clarify. "Sorry I yelled at you. I just about come undone when I saw you swingin' that maul around."

She rolled her eyes, trying to resist the urge to argue. "I wasn't swinging it around. I was bringing it down in a firm, forward motion."

It was his turn to roll his eyes. "Fine, girl, but you still wasn't bein' safe. If you'd told me you wanted to live the dream of bein' a lumberjack, I'd've shown you how."

Carefully, so as not to spook him away, she brought up her other hand to cup his cheek. "You said you were too busy to teach me things."

His eyes widened, and he seemed torn between two courses of action for a long second. Then his hand fell away, and he stepped back.

Frustrated, she grabbed a handful of his plaid shirt. "Why do you keep backing away every time I get close?"

"Why do you think, girl?" He shook his head. "This ain't never going to work. You're too young, and I'm too old."

"I don't care about age," she said softly.

He scoffed. "You just need to stop this. Ain't nothing gonna happen." Reed pulled away and turned his back to her, reaching for his coat. "Now I gotta get back to chopping wood. You sit your pretty little ass here in the house and recover."

Irritation and frustration drove her actions. With a slight wince at the stretch of the wound as she lifted her arms, Beth peeled off the camisole and threw it at him, nailing him in the back of the head.

"What the—" He broke off as he turned around to face her again, his eyes widening at the sight of her standing naked from the waist up.

"I'm not too young to know my own mind, so stop dismissing me like my desires mean nothing." Glaring at him, she kicked off her snow boots. "I'm a woman. Yeah, I'm young, but I know what I want." Her fingers shook as she unsnapped and unzipped her jeans, pushing them down to step out of them. "Who I want." Softening her tone, she said, "I want you."

His eyes narrowed, and he stormed back to her, gathering her close. "And you always get what you want, princess?"

"Always," she replied, though it felt like the wrong thing to say.

Reed growled low in his throat, and his mouth covered hers, crushing and punishing, even if it didn't frighten her. Beth threaded her fingers through his hair, dragging his head closer as his mouth ravished hers. She parted her lips, meeting his tongue enthusiastically as he kissed her in a way no man ever had before.

She turned her head, needing to draw breath. Her lips felt raw and bruised, but in a good way. He sucked on her neck before growling, "Is this what you want, princess?"

"Yes." Mostly. She wanted him, but maybe without the edge of anger.

His teeth raked her skin as he nuzzled the bend of her neck. Beth kept her hand in his hair, the other one on his waist for support. His hands were busy, one clamping around her ass, the other stroking her thigh.

"Open your legs, girl."

Responding to the command, relieved to note his tone had changed, she slid her thighs wider, so he could step between. "Reed." She moaned his name when he pressed the hard length of his arousal against her folds. His jeans and her satin underwear were barely a barrier between them.

"I'm not a toy, Beth." He said the words harshly before licking down her chest, pausing to suck on her right nipple. "You don't play with me, girl."

She shook her head, not sure if he could see from his vantage point at her breast. "I'm not. I just really want you. Have since the first day I saw you."

He made a sound that could have been a stifled groan or something expressing his disbelief. Instead of arguing or protesting, his hand slipped between their bodies, moving between her thighs. "You're gonna get me, little girl, but I hope it's what you really want." Lifting his head, his dark blue eyes drilled into hers. "I don't play sissy games or do romance. I ain't a sexy vampire, Beth. I'm the kind who bites. You may think you're gettin' what you want, but I'm the one takin'. You got that?"

She nodded, unable to speak as he pushed aside the crotch of her panties with ruthless precision, spearing her wet heat with one large finger. Beth bit her lip, moaning as he stroked her. Her thighs tightened around him, and she was thankful for the table's support. Without it, her whirling head would have sent her crashing to the ground—not to mention her knees, rendered weak by his sure strokes.

He knew exactly how to touch her, when to brush her clit, and when to penetrate her with two thick fingers. Tossing her head back, she ground against his hand, even though it hurt a little. He was awfully close to fully breaching her, and either he didn't realize or didn't care that she had never done this before. It hovered on the edge of her tongue to tell him, but the sudden way he shifted his hand, rubbing upward against her walls while circling her clit, made her almost scream.

"Let go, Beth. Come for me."

She hadn't been trying to suppress her climax, but still, his words released the floodgates. Beth arched against his hand, grinding her sex against his palm as he kept his fingers moving inside her. She clutched his shoulders hard as a powerful orgasm swept over her, making her entire body shudder.

His hand stilled, before sliding possessively to her thigh, where he gripped her leg tightly. "That's just a little taste, Beth. I'm goin' to do things to you no one ever has before."

Drawing in a shaky breath, she managed a small smile. "Shouldn't be hard. I've never let anyone get that close before."

His eyes widened, and his mercurial eyes seemed to lighten in color. A measure of tension left him, and his hold on her slackened a bit. "You're a virgin?"

Beth nodded. "It's not a big deal."

He made a sound that clearly indicated he disagreed. Shaking his head, he stepped back. "Get dressed, girl. This madness is over."

"But, Reed." Beth slid off the table, reaching for him as he took another step backward. "Please. You can't just leave it like this."

He glared at her. "I'm the one hard and aching, not you. I ain't takin' your virginity. What kind of bastard do you take me for?" He seemed angry that she was a virgin, and even angrier that she expected him not to care.

Beth wanted to continue arguing, but suddenly her mildly spinning head started whirling in earnest. "Reed, I think I'm going to faint." Before she'd even finished uttering the words, he was there, sweeping her into his arms. She didn't lose consciousness, but she did grey out for a few seconds.

When alertness returned, he was laying her on a bed, in a room she hadn't seen before. The woozy feeling made it hard to concentrate, but she assumed it was his room. Beth wanted to ask him why he'd brought her here if he had no plans to continue what they'd started in the kitchen, but she couldn't focus on calling forth the words.

He leaned over her, his face encompassing her entire world for the moment. "You need to rest now, honey. It can't be blood loss makin' you so loopy, so I'd guess shock and perhaps the demands on your body." He shook his head, looking disgusted. "Only a fool would have done what I did to you, with you hurt and all."

Beth's hand trembled as she put it on his shoulder, brushing her fingertips against the long hairs clinging to his neck. "I wanted you to. Want you still."

He seemed regretful as he stood up. "You get some rest now, Beth, and come to your senses."

She wanted to argue, to protest that her injury and the subsequent reaction hadn't been what prompted her to so boldly state her desire. Her brain was too muddled to form coherent words, and she surrendered to the urge to sleep with a small sigh, knowing nothing was resolved.

Reed waited until she was breathing deeply and checked her pulse, which was normal, before leaving his room. Only as he backed out of it, closing the door, did he realize he'd instinctively brought her down the hallway to his personal space. It wouldn't have taken more than another minute to put her in the guestroom, but he'd followed his gut.

She sure had looked good lying on his bed, those pale blonde tresses a beautiful contrast to the serviceable navy bedding set. He cursed aloud as he moved from the door, hating what he'd let happen in the kitchen.

No, that wasn't true. He'd enjoyed it right up to the point he'd discovered she was a virgin, though anger had fueled his original response. He'd reacted blindly, hating that the spoiled rich girl thought he was just another thing she could acquire, that her wants were so important that everyone should fall in line. His pulse had still been racing from the shock of seeing her with that maul, followed by her injury, and it had all overwhelmed his common sense.

He'd touched her when he knew better, and the rest of his intentions had gone up in smoke. Anger and desire still thrummed through him, making his heart beat loudly in his ears and his dick hard to the point of pain. Another few minutes of touching her hot pussy, and he'd have come in his pants just thinking about being inside her.

"Fuckin' virgin," he said aloud, disgruntled. The fifteen years separating them had been bad enough, not to mention their life experiences and backgrounds. But taking her innocence wasn't something he could do. Might as well tattoo "dirty old bastard" on his forehead and get it over with if he did. He'd see the phantom words every time he looked at himself in the mirror, with or without the ink.

"Damn girl." Reed adjusted the snug fit of his pants, cursing her for making him want things he knew he couldn't have. For making him want her, the type of woman who should never appeal to a man who'd been on the receiving end of hauteur and disdain from her kind most of his life, 'til he came to Alaska. Here, folks didn't much care where you came from, or what haunted you, long as you kept to yourself. He'd just have to make sure he kept to himself and stayed away from her.

As he redressed in his coat to return to the woodshed, he shot a dour glare at the gray sky. "And don't even think about snowin' again, you sumbitch."

Chapter Five

BETH WASN'T SURE HOW long she'd slept, but she woke feeling both better and worse. Her head was clearer, and that awful shaky, dizzy feeling had passed. On the other hand, her chest ached where the ax had split her skin, and she rubbed around the spot, hoping to dispel some discomfort. As she did so, she noticed Reed had put the camisole back on her at some point.

He was nowhere to be seen, but she stretched to turn on the lamp, whimpering at a hot pain shooting through her cut as she did so. The illumination lit up the room, except for the dimmest corners, verifying he wasn't there.

With interest, she looked around his room, finding it neat and tidy, but lacking almost all traces of personal touches. The walls were paneled wood, and the navy carpet matched the bedding. A serviceable dresser made from raw timber, complete with knotholes and whirls, was in the corner. A massive stone fireplace made up one wall, complete with the seemingly standard-issue fur rug before it. The only personal mark he'd added was a bookshelf in the same kind of wood, filled with an assortment of paperbacks, and one row of hardbacks.

Moving slowly, she eased out of bed, stopping first to seek out the facilities. Selecting the door that didn't lead to the hallway, she found a small bathroom, similar in design and dimensions to the one in the guest quarters. After taking care of practicalities, she returned to his room and went to the bookshelf, perusing the choices. There was an eclectic mix of bestsellers, horror, mysteries, a few nonfiction titles, and even a couple of romances.

The sight of a photo album crammed in the corner of the bottom shelf, beside a hardback copy of one of Stephen King's novels, caught her attention. Feeling a little guilty, she bent down to pick it up, wincing at the stretching in her chest. Clasping the book under her right arm, she returned to the bed, taking a moment to bury her face in the pillow to inhale his scent. It was earthy and male, both raw and sweet.

With a small sigh, she positioned the pillows behind her and put the album on her lap. She flipped through the pages, finding most empty. There were some of him as a younger man, and even a few as a kid, though no baby pictures. She saw a few pictures of a little girl who shared similar features. The last page was a picture of Reed in his Army uniform, surrounded by eight guys. Some of them stood at attention, but a few were laughing, or just turning their head in a way that suggested this picture had been shot immediately after a formal pose.

Her heart melted at the big grin on his face. He looked younger, of course, and more carefree, as though not as much had weighed him down. Beth didn't know a lot about the Army or squads, but she assumed the men surrounding him were his comrades who had fallen in Kandahar.

The door opened, and she looked up from the photo album to see Reed entering with a tray in his hand. It was an incongruously domestic sight, especially with the younger, military image of him still in her mind. She offered a tentative smile. "Hello."

He inclined his head, his expression hard to read. "Thought you might be hungry."

Her stomach rumbled in reply, and she nodded. "Starved."

Reed frowned as he set the tray on the nightstand. "Snoopin' through my stuff, girl?"

"Yep," she admitted, unabashed. He'd brought her to his room, so that was an invitation, of sorts. "You looked good in your uniform."

He ignored the compliment to lift the book from her lap. At first, she thought he was angry, but then his lips quirked into a small smile at the picture of him and his buddies. "Those were some good times. Hard, but good. We was close, just like family." Reed touched the edge of the picture for a moment. "That squad was like my brothers."

Hesitantly, she reached out to touch his hip, the only part easy to reach. "Are they the ones...?"

He nodded, his expression aloof for a moment. "It was an ambush. They all died."

She'd already conveyed her condolences the first time he'd mentioned them, so she offered an awkward pat instead. He endured it for a moment before stepping away from her to take the album back to the shelf. As he slipped it into its spot, she said, "You were a cute kid."

He turned to walk back toward her, grinning. "I'm still cute."

Her lips twitched. "I'd concede that." She lifted the tray from the nightstand to put on her lap. "You're spoiling me." Something unpleasant flickered across his face, as though he wanted to make a snide remark, but he didn't comment. The aroma of the leftover stew teased her nostrils, and she inhaled deeply before taking a big bite. It was even better than the first day.

"So, who's the girl in the album?" she asked as she chewed the bite of stew.

Reed frowned, but finally answered. "My sister."

"Older or younger?"

"Older."

He was just a font of information. "Where does she live?"

"Don't know." He had that surly look again and spoke with a finality that transmitted he was done discussing his sibling. His eyes practically dared her to ask why he didn't know where the other woman lived.

Beth decided to try steering the conversation down a different track. "You don't have any pictures of your parents?"

His mouth curled. "Why the hell would I want those, girl?" Reed practically snarled, "Waste of space."

"In the album?"

He nodded. "Album and life, they was both a waste of space."

"Are they still alive?"

Abruptly, his expression darkened. "What's with the interrogation?"

Beth drew back a bit. "Sorry. I was just trying to get to know you."

He shook his head. "You don't gotta get to know me. All you gotta do is eat your food and get your ass outta my bed."

Moisture pricked her eyes, but she didn't let it fall. Silly of her, but she'd thought they had made headway earlier in the day, that intimacy was a foregone conclusion. Getting better acquainted had seemed a good way to facilitate that, but he'd practically slammed the door shut in her face.

Setting the spoon back in the bowl, she put the tray on the nightstand. Anger spurred her from the bed. "I don't need to finish my dinner first. You're welcome to your bed right now." Waving at it, she added, "I don't even know why *you* put me in it to start with, Reed."

His cheeks took on a ruddy hue, and he couldn't seem to meet her eyes. "Was closer is all."

She scoffed and marched past him, trying not to show she was a bit intimidated to be clad only in the satin camisole and matching white panties. Her pants were MIA, and the sweater had a hole in it. Since she was too angry to even consider asking him to borrow a robe, or go get some of her clothes, she'd just have to make do with her underwear and be grateful she wasn't bare-ass naked.

"You forgot your food."

Beth was too annoyed to feel even a bit hungry right then. With a rude gesture in his direction, she stalked from his room, slamming the door behind her, and hurried to the room she was using in his house. If she hadn't been surrounded by snow and darkness, she would have packed her bag and left right then. He could go screw himself. That was as close as he was going to get to any action while there were just the two of them in the house.

She didn't bother to change as she slid into bed. Huddled under the thick covers in the guestroom, she stared at the screen of her e-reader without actually absorbing any of the words. The harsh sound of the wind gusting outside only deepened her misery and left her feeling more alone than she'd ever been. A peek out the window showed snow coming down so thickly that she couldn't make out anything but a blur. It seemed like a blizzard out there.

Disappointment left a bitter taste in her mouth. She'd really misjudged Reed, thinking there was a softer side to him. The flashes of sweetness that occasionally shone through his surly exterior had misled her. That, and her own hormones, which still clamored for him—though she was so angry that her mind wanted nothing to do with him.

She glared at the foul weather, guessing it would keep her father and his film crew from arriving for at least a couple more days. Beth planned to get on that plane when it headed back to Endline, or whatever hole-in-the-wall it went to next. If she had her way, the wheels would barely touch the landing strip before she'd be on it, waiting for takeoff. The idea of spending some time with her dad while he might be a semi-captive audience was already a bust, and she sure wasn't sticking around when the opportunity to escape presented itself. It wasn't as though Blair Wyndam would notice her absence anyway. He'd barely masked his impatience at having to deal with her unexpected arrival.

A tear streaked down her cheek then, and she swiped it away. By now, she should be used to his brusqueness and lack of attention. Her mother had tried to gently dissuade her from the "surprise," but Beth had ignored her advice to wait for a better time. There was never a better time with her father.

Maybe that's why she was taking Reed's behavior so badly. It was just another rejection. God, did she have Daddy Issues that she was trying to work out by getting attention from an older man? The thought turned her stomach, and she quickly shook her head, knowing that wasn't true. Whatever drew her to Reed—and it sure wasn't his charming personality or sunny disposition—had nothing to do with him being remotely father-figure-like. She wanted him in a purely female fashion, the way a woman wanted a lover, not a father. There was nothing muddled about her feelings. It was lust, pure and simple.

How could it be anything else? Reed would clearly never open up to her, and she was done extending overtures toward him. She would move on, consign this interlude to a distant place in her memory, and keep looking for a man who made her body sing the same way he did. She squashed the voice at the back of her head whispering that no other man had ever made her feel this way before. Of course they hadn't. She was only eighteen. There was plenty of time to find someone who came close enough.

That thought was dissatisfying, and she tried to clear it, and all the other thoughts, from her mind. Putting aside the e-reader, she turned off the lamp and lay down. There was still some light from the alarm clock on the nightstand, enough to reassure her she wasn't in total darkness, so she closed her eyes, breathed deeply, and halfway mediated herself to a light sleep.

She awoke sometime later from a nightmare she barely remembered. Instinctively, her eyes sought a source of light, but found none. Beth fumbled for her phone or e-reader, knowing either would give her some illumination, but couldn't find them in the dark. Her hand brushed against something on the nightstand and sent it crashing to the floor.

Still somewhat caught up in her dream, combined with the total darkness and the fierce sounds from outside, she panicked. Beth thrashed around in search of her phone or e-reader, irrationally fearing getting out of bed to try to feel for whichever she had dropped on the floor. Her hand connected with the lamp and sent it flying. It hit the wall with a crashing sound that made her cry out with surprise.

Torn between the need for light and the need to hide, she huddled back under the blankets and tried to calm her racing heart. Cautiously, she extended a hand from the covers, groping on the nightstand until she finally recognized the shape of her phone. Clutching it like a lifeline, she swiped the screen just as her door crashed open.

Beth screamed, pressing herself against the headboard, while holding the phone out as though it would ward off her attacker.

"It's me," said Reed, sounding gruff.

Her thundering pulse slowed, and she dragged in a deep breath. A second later, she was vaguely aware of the bed dipping as he sat down beside her, but she was still too caught up in the aftereffects of fear to either welcome him or tell him to go away. With bald honesty, she admitted she didn't want him to leave. The presence of anyone soothed her frazzled nerves, but she had to acknowledge that having him beside her brought a greater measure of comfort than anyone else she could think of at the moment.

His hand was gentle on her upper arm. "You okay?"

Beth nodded, not sure if he could see the motion in the dark room. His flashlight, added with her phone, still provided only meager lighting. "Why's it so dark?" The pathetic tone made her cringe.

"The storm probably knocked out the main power. The genny should kick on soon. It's programmed to start if primary power don't come back within forty-five minutes."

She trembled, imagining being without lights for that long. "Why the wait?"

"Conserve fuel."

Beth swallowed, her throat feeling arid. "So, you just sit in the dark for all that time, waiting?"

"There's candles and such." He leaned closer, and though his expression wasn't visible, his tone sounded gentle. "You don't gotta be scared of the dark, Beth."

She nodded again. "I know, but it's a bit of a phobia." Biting her lip, knowing he probably didn't care, she found herself sharing anyway. "I played hide-and-seek with some friends when I was about six. I sneaked up to the attic and found a great hiding place in an old trunk." She shivered, remembering the fear of being in that small box that had let in only a tiny sliver of light. "The problem was, the latch was broken, and it didn't open from the inside. I was trapped in there for a long time."

He exhaled loudly. "How long?"

She lifted a shoulder. "I don't know. Hours, maybe a day. No one even realized I was missing until my mom came home from a shopping trip." Beth's mouth curled. "Dad was home, but he was too busy with something to notice. Probably my nanny." He took her hand in his, and she squeezed gratefully. "That's just a guess, but I know I had a new nanny two days later, so she was either fired for incompetence or for being one of my dad's affairs. Or both."

Beth took a couple of deep breaths before loosening her hold on his hand. To her surprise, he didn't release her, even when she tried to tug away. "Anyway, I'm fine now. I woke up from a bad dream to all this darkness, and it made me panic. Needlessly." Her voice wobbled just a bit when she asked, "I wouldn't say no to one of those candles, if it isn't too much bother, before you go back to bed?"

He let out a ragged sigh. "Of course it ain't too much trouble, Beth." The bed shifted as he stretched across her, his chest pressing against her shoulder, to reach into the drawer of the nightstand. Holding up his flashlight, he showed her the two candles and the lighter he'd retrieved from the drawer. "But I ain't leaving you like this. You're clearly still scared."

Another shiver ran through her, as though to prove his point. "I'm not scared, Reed. Just a little rattled still." She didn't exactly encourage him to leave as he lit the candles, providing more light, though shadows still dominated the room. She shivered again when he returned to an upright position beside her.

The fear had faded, and the realization that he was in her room, with only a few layers of clothes and her blankets separating them, hit her. Beth gulped quietly, torn between anxiety, anticipation, and some of her lingering anger from his earlier behavior.

A loud crash distracted her from all her conflicting emotions, making her cry out and cling to him, just like some dumb heroine in one of those old scary movies. Tears rushed from her eyes, and she couldn't completely identify why she was crying. All she knew was the fear from being in darkness had left her raw and exposed. Sniffing hard, she made an effort to rein in her emotions, certain Reed had to be uncomfortable with the display—though he had wrapped his arms around her and pulled her closer, instead of pushing her away or holding himself stiffly aloof from her.

She swallowed and spoke as soon as she could. "Sorry. I think the whole experience has left me freaked out. I'm not the crying type." Beth didn't try to see his expression in the gloom, not wanting to read skepticism in his gaze. She truly wasn't used to crying. With the exception of the traumatic experience of being locked in the attic, the death of her favorite horse when she was eleven, and the passing of her grandfather two years ago, she couldn't remember crying about much of anything.

"It's okay, girl. Sometimes, you just need a good cry." He rubbed his palm over her back in a circular motion.

She giggled, which sounded a bit wet, but relieved most of her remaining tension. "Yeah, I'm sure you cry all the time, Reed."

A trace of amusement touched his words. "Hell yeah. I get out the bonbons and pop in a *Lifetime* move at least twice a month."

She laughed harder. "You don't have any bonbons."

"'Course not. I ate 'em all."

Before she could reply, the same crashing sound jarred her again, and she jumped. "What is that?"

"Sounds like one of the shutters blew open. I can go close it."

"No." She tightened her arms instinctively, knowing if he left now, he wouldn't be back. His version of common sense would have a chance to take hold, and he'd talk himself into staying away from her. "That's okay," she said more softly. "I don't want to be alone yet."

"All right."

Silence fell between them, but he didn't move farther away. His hand continued the same circuitous route across her back, and she continued to cling to him. Beth realized he was grasping her hip almost hard enough to hurt, but she made no move to wiggle away. They were frozen in a single minute, and the wrong move could end everything. The trouble was, she didn't know what the wrong move was. Or the right one. He'd rejected her overtures too many times for her to feel secure enough to attempt to initiate anything.

"I should go," he whispered, though he didn't move.

"No," she said again.

"You still scared, girl?"

"No," she whispered, and she didn't even twitch when the shutter crashed against the house again.

"I am," he said in a hoarse whisper.

Beth stiffened, raising her head enough to try to see his features in the gloom. "What? Why?"

"You're dangerous." He jerked his head in the direction of the window. "Lot more dangerous than that storm out there."

Beth licked her lips, uncertain about the right words, which was an unusual affliction for her. "I promise not to kung fu you."

"I wish you would." His hand stopped moving in circles and began applying pressure to her upper back, urging her closer. "Knock some sense into me."

Feeling a bit more confident, Beth tangled a hand in his overlong hair. "I don't want you to be sensible, Reed. I just want to feel."

"Feel what?" He sounded as uncertain as her.

"This." She put a hand over his heart, finding it beating strong and steady against her palm. "You. Everything."

"You're a virgin. You deserve better'n some dirty old bastard for your first time, honey."

Beth laughed softly, letting her hand slide lower, to rest across his flat stomach. "You don't feel old." She sniffed his chest, inhaling his heavenly masculine scent. "You don't smell dirty." Leaning a bit closer, she rested her head on his chest. "And I couldn't care less if your parents were married."

He stiffened for a long second, and she cursed herself for mentioning the obviously forbidden subject. Then he relaxed and pulled her closer. "Guess I'm not a bastard in the technical sense, in that case."

"Then what's the problem?" she whispered against his neck.

"Too many to count," he muttered. "Ah, hell, math never was my strong point."

Beth had no time to savor her victory as he lifted her onto his lap, his mouth slanting over hers possessively. He kissed her deeply, with fervor that matched her own. Their tongues tangled and collided, almost as if they were at war. Perhaps it was a bit like a battle, since she wanted to breach his walls and claim a piece of him for herself.

His kisses slowed slightly, becoming long and drugging, as his hands pushed up her camisole to caress her stomach and back. Beth let her own hands roam freely, pleased to find he'd come to her in nothing but boxer shorts. Turning her head slightly, she asked, "Do you sleep in these?"

"Nah. I just grabbed the first thing in the drawer when I heard you scream."

"I think I'd like you better without them." Beth slipped her hands inside the waistband to stroke his hips, inching down the underwear as she did so. He groaned and thrust against her, letting her feel the full length of his arousal against her heated flesh. Motivated, she gave up her efforts to tug them down and sought out her prize. Reed groaned when she wrapped her hand around his cock, squeezing gently. "Hmm, much better," she managed to say, though her mind was a bit fragmented, between the pleasure of touching him and the tingles shooting through her body from his hands cradling her breasts.

Reed thrust against her hand as he pulled the camisole off, carefully maneuvering around her wound. His mouth kissed a wide circle around the bandage. "You almost stopped my heart this afternoon. 'Bout keeled over when I saw you bleedin.'"

"It didn't show. You handled it easily."

He shook his head, his hair tickling her chest. "Not on the inside. It left me off-kilter. Guess that's why you was able to seduce me so easy."

Beth laughed. "I've been planning to since a few minutes after I got off the plane."

He snorted. "Still don't believe that."

Annoyed, she put her hands around his cheeks, forcing his head up from her cleavage. "I'm not lying. I try never to lie." For emphasis, she kissed him again, sliding her tongue along the bottom of his lip before pushing inside. Beth clung to him, not breaking the kiss, as he shifted their positions so she was lying under him. He let her control the kiss for a minute, before taking over, thrusting his tongue inside her mouth and leaving her breathless.

She closed her eyes, losing herself in his touch as his mouth drifted lower. He paused for a leisurely, thorough inspection of her breasts, pushing them together so his tongue could alternate between her nipples. Beth had never much enjoyed nipple stimulation, but perhaps it had more to do with the technique of the two boys who'd gone before, because this man had her writhing and thrusting against him.

Calling out his name, she wrapped her thighs around his waist, rubbing her pussy against his stomach. "I need you, Reed."

"Shush, girl, I'm comin'." He chuckled against her stomach. "Or you are, soon enough."

Beth drew in her breath, holding it with anticipation and a touch of fear as he neared the apex of her thighs. None of her boyfriends had ever gotten so close before, and they'd certainly never done that. "Oh, god." Had he swiped the side of his tongue down her? Or maybe the flat part? "Oh, Reed, that's..." She trailed off, unable to speak again as breathless moans escaped her. His mouth moved with deliberate purpose, and he was clearly skilled. When he added his fingers to the mix, she lost control and came with a sob, calling out his name as her body shivered and jerked underneath him. It made the orgasm he'd given her earlier in the day seem almost mild by comparison, and she was embarrassed to find she was riding his face like a thing possessed as he kept licking, eliciting another orgasm before he lifted his head.

When she could breathe, she reached out a shaky hand to touch his shoulder. "I've never done it before, but do you want me to...?"

He shook his head. "Not tonight. I just wanna be inside your pussy." He wriggled a finger still in her passage. "You're so fuckin' tight."

She licked her lips. "Have you ever been with a virgin before?"

Reed was close enough now that she could see his expression—one of consternation, with perhaps a touch of guilt. "Never."

"You prefer the experienced type?" Insecurities flooded her, and she loosened her thighs.

"The only type I got is the type that wants a good, hard fuck, Beth."

She barely held in the shudder that tried to escape. "Well, I want that."

"That ain't what you want." He pushed hair out of his eyes impatiently. "You want sweet 'n tender, and you deserve it. Your first time should be special."

Sensing he was on the verge of changing his mind, she resorted to dirty tactics. Sliding lower, she cupped his erection in her hand. "This feels special to me."

He groaned as she moved her grip down his shaft and up again. "A good guy'd do the right thing here."

"You feel good to me." She hoped he knew she meant that on more than just a physical level. Reed was surly and rough, but she was sure there was a good, caring man underneath that exterior. He wore it like a shell, in much the same way she wore her cheerful mask that hid any hurts her father's negligence caused.

"I ain't good, 'cause I ain't walkin' away." He pulled away long enough to remove his underwear, allowing her time to do the same. When Reed returned to her, he seemed to have a new sense of purpose as he started touching and kissing her again. His cock nestled against her slick folds, and she lifted her hips, wanting him inside her.

"Please, Reed." She whimpered when his head pushed inside her, but barely stifled a curse when he pulled away. "What?" Beth flinched when he cursed. "Did I do something wrong?"

He shook his head. "Nah, it ain't you. I can't do this."

She did curse then, beyond frustrated. "I don't know how many ways there are to tell you I want you to fuck me, Reed. I don't give a damn that you're fifteen years older, or a grumpy dick most of the time. I want you."

To her surprise, he chuckled. "Good to know where I stand, girl." His expression revealed his own frustration. "It ain't that. I ain't got protection."

"Oh. Ohhh." Beth struggled with dates, mentally calculating. "It's not a problem."

He sagged a bit. "Thank god, girl, 'cause the only way my balls would get any bluer is if I dunked 'em in a snow bank."

She laughed as he returned to her, nudging her legs apart. "You're a silver-tongued devil, Reed."

"I can be." He aligned his cock with her delicate tissue. "Maybe you need a reminder?"

She shook her head. "Not right now. I just need you." Tightening her legs around him, she lifted upward as he settled inside her tight passage. Beth winced a bit at the stretching feeling, but it didn't hurt.

He held himself on his hands, clearly trying to avoid crushing her. "You okay?"

She nodded. "I thought there would be pain, but it's just a little uncomfortable." When he pulled back to sink in again, she experienced another twinge, but that soon faded. His fingers dancing across her clit, coupled with the perfect way his cock pushed against a sensitive spot inside her, soon catapulted her straight into ecstasy, and she didn't have the ability to worry about her technique or be more than a little concerned that she was being too enthusiastic as she bucked against him, straining for every inch he gave her.

She gripped his shoulders with so much pressure she thought her nails were leaving marks. Rather than loosen her hold, she applied a bit more, liking, on a primal level, the idea of marking him. He was her man, and she wanted to leave proof.

Even primal thoughts fled as her orgasm crested, crashing over her and making her convulse and cry out. Reed's muscles tightened, and he went rigid against her as his seed spilled inside her. He buried his mouth against her throat, biting her gently as he came, leaving territorial marks of his own.

Reed woke later to the blissful sensation of wet heat sliding up and down his cock. He groaned when she licked the head of his shaft before sucking again. He closed his eyes as she took care of him. Considering she'd never done it before, his girl had talent.

His eyes popped open at the thought. "No," he said harshly, and she froze. He'd been talking to himself, denying that she was "his" girl. Beth wasn't his and never would be. Once the weather cleared, and Wyndam was done with his documentary, she'd be gone forever. A groan of reluctance left him when she withdrew her mouth, and he frowned at the uncertainty in her voice.

"I'm sorry if I did something wrong." She sounded shaky, and a touch shy, when she added, "I just wanted to give you some of what you gave me."

"You didn't do nothing wrong, Beth." He reached for her, drawing her close for a deep kiss before speaking again. "You were doin' a good job. Too good. I didn't wanna come in your mouth."

"Oh." She slid across him, straddling him with her opening poised over the head of his shaft. "Do you want to come somewhere else then?"

With a growl, he cupped her ass in his hands, pushing her down on him forcefully, but with care to ensure he didn't hurt her tender passageway. "That's the spot." He thrust against her as she rode him, his hands guiding her movements as he surged deeply inside her, making her moan and cry out.

Her pussy tightened around him just before she came, and he gritted his teeth to hold on to his own release so she could let go first. She cried his name in a breathless way that sent a pang through his chest. As he spilled his seed inside her, he couldn't deny the knowledge that he wanted to claim her, to make her his woman.

It was only after the euphoria faded that he remembered all the reasons that couldn't happen. Pulling her against him, pressing a kiss to the top of her head, he hoped she was thinking of all those reasons too. The last thing he needed was to have to discourage her from having feelings for him. It was difficult enough forcing himself to keep a distance without having to worry about her emotions too.

Chapter Six

HE'D LEFT MORE THAN a few marks on her in the past few days, Beth thought with a pleased smile, eyeing the hickeys, scratches, and light bruises garnered from vigorous sex. He couldn't seem to help himself, as though driven to leave his mark on her. It felt possessive and territorial, and she loved it, even though it wasn't politically correct to think that way.

Still standing in front of the mirror, she zipped her pants and reached for a sweater. It was the first time in three days, since the night she'd become his lover, that she'd had any reason to dress or get out of bed for more than a few minutes. The weather had raged on for most of the time, making it impossible for her father and his crew to arrive. They'd taken advantage of the interlude to get better acquainted.

At least physically, she thought with a small sigh, as she slipped on her sweater. She knew every inch of Reed's body by now, and had a fair idea how to drive him wild, but she was no closer to knowing the man. He didn't rebuff her questions so harshly now, but he didn't answer either. She'd talked and chatted, telling him every inane detail of her life in hopes he would open up, but she'd gotten nothing. "Blue," she muttered. He'd told her his favorite color yesterday. What a breakthrough.

He was waiting for her in the kitchen, having promised her a walk. Actually, having insisted she get out of his bed, leave the roaring fire, and come with him so she could get some exercise. He'd ignored her protests that she'd gotten a lot of exercise the past few days, before admitting that he'd never get out and see to the chores if he knew she was lying in bed waiting for him.

So here she was, ready to tackle the great outdoors, post-whiteout. The chime of her phone distracted her from her own face in the mirror, and she reached for it, pleasantly surprised to find service restored. The text was from her mom, decrying how an early period had ruined her spa trip.

Beth giggled as she sent her sympathies, wondering if it had interfered with her mother's planned treatments, or something more sensual with one of guests. Or an employee. Her mother wasn't hung up on social status and remained unbothered by little details, such as fidelity to a dead marriage.

Feeling a twinge of sadness that her mother had settled for such a sad union, she put down the phone, her gaze falling on the calendar as she did. Something niggled in the back of her brain, and she scooped up the phone again. Opening the app, she looked at her calendar, certain she had forgotten something. Seeing no urgent appointments for the remainder of February, she swiped to go to March. What was bothering her hit her when she saw the tiny flower.

Going back to the previous screen, Beth found the flower in February, releasing a ragged exhalation when the date didn't match what she'd calculated. How could she have made such a mistake? From the time she was twelve and got her first cycle, she'd had a period every twenty-nine days. Her last cycle had been as consistent as usual, but she'd somehow added a week to the date she'd started in her mental calculations the other night.

Feeling a bit weak, Beth collapsed on the bed in the guestroom, where all her things remained, though she had spent most of the last three days with Reed in his room. Three of her most fertile days. "Holy hell." How had she messed up so badly? Had her brain been too fogged with passion to remember the right date, or had she deliberately let herself "forget" so she wouldn't have to tell Reed it wasn't safe to proceed?

She squirmed, remembering how she had told him she never lied. Would he believe it had been an honest mistake, or would he assume she'd lied deliberately? Her stomach twisted as she imagined the ugly things he might say if he thought she'd been trying to trap him into something.

Maybe she was overreacting. Even though she was young, and probably fertile, that didn't mean she was absolutely going to get pregnant from the sex they'd had the past three days. It was stupid to freak out about it right now, when she couldn't do anything to change the outcome anyway. Emergency contraception was about as reachable as the moon in the current environment, and they were already past her most fertile window. There was no reason to stop their intimacies now. What was that saying? It'd be like closing the stall after the horse ran away? Something like that.

She just wouldn't say anything for now, until she knew there was a reason to have to. Abruptly, she remembered her half-sister, Megan, had struggled with infertility. She was a decade older than Beth, but she'd still been just twenty-five when she'd started trying with her husband. It had taken almost two years and three IVF cycles for them to conceive their twins. It boded well for her odds of not getting pregnant the first time if her half-sister had trouble conceiving. Didn't it? She clung to that hope as she put away the phone.

Struggling to compose herself, she took a deep breath, unable to suppress the wave of guilt. She hadn't deliberately misled Reed, but it still felt dishonest, especially since she wasn't sharing her concerns. As much as she wanted to pretend it was solely to spare him worrying for two weeks before they could discover if they were going to be parents, she knew she was afraid to confess. He didn't seem like he would be happy with the idea, and he was probably going to assume the worst of her. Was it wrong to cost herself another few days in his arms? Should she waste the opportunity to get better acquainted with him by ruining the remainder of their time together?

Sickened by herself, she looked away, no longer able to meet her own eyes. It was wrong not to tell him, not to warn him, but she couldn't make herself do the right thing here. Was this how her father had started becoming such a selfish person, consumed with his own needs to the exclusion of being able to consider others'? Had it been one small step down a slippery slope? Was she going to turn out like Blair?

Reed's voice interrupted her mental castigations. "Get your ass movin', girl. You're burnin' daylight."

She rolled her eyes as she went into the kitchen, briefly glad he didn't know her well enough to tell she was upset. "Funny." The pale light wouldn't appreciably change for a while.

He smacked her bottom as she went past him before handing her an apple. "Here."

She almost drooled. "Fresh fruit? Way up here, in the middle of winter?"

He laughed. "The root cellar keeps them real nice."

She took a bite, finding it still crisp and tart. "Yum."

After her impromptu breakfast of apple and Reed's kisses, they left the cabin. She trudged around behind him, finding the snowshoes he'd given her awkward. Of course, he moved as though he'd been born wearing them. She was huffing and puffing by the time they stopped at the shed housing the generators. Beth leaned against a table as he checked everything, topped off the fuel in one, and wrote something on a pad on the table.

"Looks good." He rubbed his gloved hands together, as if to generate warmth, while he led her from the shed.

"Are we done?" She shivered in the cold.

"Nope. Gotta check the snowmobiles."

With a sigh, she followed him to another small shed. "Why don't you keep all these together?"

He opened the door and stepped inside the small room, which allowed no space for her. "Couple reasons. If the weather causes one of the buildings to cave in or somethin', I got a spare genny in each of the others. If something happens to make the generators blow, or they catch fire, I don't lose my only transportation in the process, keepin' the snowmobiles separate."

She nodded. "That's smart. I'm not sure I'd have thought of that."

He grinned. "You gotta think about everything livin' out here. 'Course, I read books and talked to locals before buying this place and gettin' started."

"How did you end up here?" she asked as he nodded his satisfaction with the snowmobiles and closed the shed door.

He looked haunted for a moment, and she was sure he wouldn't answer, so it was a surprise when he said, "After Kandahar, I was lost. The Army said I wasn't fit to serve no more." He tapped his head, looking disgusted. "Nutjob, though they call it PTSD."

She frowned. "That's not a nutjob. It's real."

He shrugged, as though he wanted to dismiss the subject. "Yeah, it's real, but I didn't need no damn shrink probin' my life. I kicked around a bit before I found myself working on a fishin' boat one summer in Alaska."

She struggled to keep up with him as he set off toward the direction of the runway. He moved quickly, and she didn't know if it was his natural pace, or just his instinctive urge to flee the conversation. "How did you like that?"

Reed snorted. "It's hard, disgustin' work. Don't leave much time for a man to get all introspective and dwell on how he's the only survivor of his squad." He shrugged again. "They ought to make it therapy for all PTSD cases. Did me a world o' good. Bit like an emotional enema." He laughed, though it held a sharp edge. "Once I got rid of the baggage from the Army, I was ready for something else. Alaska calls to me, so I stayed." They stopped near the runway, and cursed. "I'm definitely going to have to plow this shit before the group arrives. Not that I'd expect them to dig their way out at Endline for another couple days at least."

Her heart lifted at the thought of having two more days alone with him, but it didn't make her lose track of their conversation. "How'd you end up going from fisherman to guide and owning all this?"

"Hard work. Lived on beans and salmon I caught myself, scraped together a down payment, used my VA benefits to finance the place, and sunk everything I have into it."

From his expression, she didn't think he meant just financially. This place owned Reed's soul. Probably his heart too, which made it doubtful that he had much room left for anyone inside it. Could he ever love her—any woman—as much as he loved this land?

Their conversation ended suddenly as they came upon a gruesome sight. Beth rushed forward, ignoring his warning to be careful as she knelt beside a white fox. It was obvious the poor thing was dead, having been caught in a trap that it must have dragged with it. Out of desperation, it must have tried to chew off its paw and had bled out. Tears came to her eyes. "How is this fair or sportsmanlike, Reed? Traps are cowardly."

He nodded. "There's some people that live around this area that don't give a damn about property lines or cruelty."

She sniffed. "The trap isn't yours?"

His blue eyes darkened. "Hell no, it ain't mine. I wouldn't leave any animal to suffer for days with these damn things. It ain't no kind of way to hunt. You don't know what you're gonna catch, or how long it'll be here. Most of 'em die from starvation or dehydration." He shook his head, his gaze softening with pity as it fell on the ravaged fox's leg. "Or blood loss."

Tentatively, she touched his leg. "I'm sorry. I shouldn't have just assumed—"

He nodded, looking pacified for a moment, until he knelt closer to the fox. "Dammit."

"What?"

"She died with milk." At her blink of incomprehension, he said, "She's got babies somewhere. Probably dead by now, but we gotta look."

At that moment, seeing the rough-edged, pragmatic hunter gearing up to find orphaned baby foxes, her heart melted, and the truth struck her like a bludgeon. She'd fallen completely head-over-heels in love with the man. Beth didn't know whether to be happy or terrified. He was tender and caring, but he was also stubborn and closed off. It seemed impossible she could ever penetrate his walls and get him to feel anything even close to love for her.

She tried to push aside her thoughts and pay attention to the instructions he gave her. They didn't split up, though she thought he might have suggested it if she'd been more experienced in the outdoors, and she did her best not to slow him down.

His persistence paid off as he found a small den in a rotted log within forty minutes. Beth didn't protest when he insisted on checking it out, not wanting to find a den of dead babies. Finding their poor mother had been traumatic enough. He lived a hard life, in conditions she'd never imagined before coming here. How could she ever fit into it? Would he even want her to? There had been no mention of anything long-term between them. Until her epiphany a little while ago, she'd had herself convinced this was nothing more than her first affair, that she would regretfully part from Reed in a couple of weeks and look back with fond memories—assuming she wasn't left with a permanent memento of their relationship.

Being highly educated didn't exempt one from being stupid sometimes, she conceded. Reed, with his most likely no more than high school education, had probably already figured out the complications that could ensue from having an affair with a virgin. He'd no doubt been concerned about her getting all clingy and emotional, which must have been part of why he'd held back. She didn't think they would be lovers now if events hadn't brought them together, barely dressed, in the same bed, in the middle of the night. By the light of day, he'd have talked himself out of doing something as dumb as risking making a virgin fall for him.

Her thoughts scattered when he scooted backward and stood up, cradling something in his hands. "Is it a baby?"

He nodded. "The only one, as far as I can tell. Looks maybe four weeks, so she might have cycled out of season and had a small litter." Reed cuddled the fox closer to him. "Foxes can come into heat any time, but most kits are born in spring."

"What will you do with it?"

He stuffed the fox down his shirt, and it whimpered weakly. "First thing to do is see if we can keep it alive. After that, I'll contact a wildlife rescue and rehabilitation center my friend runs, once the weather settles down."

They hurried back to the cabin, her hips and back protesting the last few steps in the wretched snowshoes. It was a relief to take them off, along with the rest of her outdoor gear. Reed slipped off his coat and immediately moved into the great room, where he'd left a fire banked. Beth took the baby awkwardly when he handed it over.

"Put it in your shirt. Your skin'll help warm it up."

Beth did as he suggested as Reed brought the fire to life, instantly providing welcome warmth. "What are you going to feed him?" Somehow, she wouldn't have been surprised to find he kept a stock of wildlife formula, since he seemed to have everything else one might need out here.

He disappointed her with his pragmatic answer. "I'm thinkin' sweetened condensed milk for the first few feedings, to give the critter some energy. After that, he'll have to settle for evaporated milk or powdered, plus meat." He stared at the kit. "I think he might be able to handle a morsel of meat once he gets some calories in 'im. A bit young maybe, but he won't make it if we don't try."

Beth wanted to hand the baby over to Reed right then. Not because she didn't care about it, but because she was afraid she'd grow too attached. Still, she let the little furball nuzzle against her chest as he busied himself in the kitchen, preparing the meager meal for the new arrival.

That first feeding, watching the little one struggle to eat, she was sure he wouldn't last the night. The second feeding, two hours later, was just as hard, but he seemed to have adapted to the eyedropper by the third feeding. She took a feeding the next time, allowing Reed to rest, before he sent her back for a nap.

When she woke later the next morning, it was to the welcome sight of more snow falling. Very welcome, because it meant more time with just the two of them. Well, three of them, counting the kit.

Beth slipped on a robe over her pajamas for the warmth before leaving the guestroom to check on the orphan. She had briefly considered the idea of sleeping in Reed's bed last night, but he hadn't offered. Since he wasn't going to be beside her, she'd forced herself to take the guestroom, not wanting him to think she was clingy or needy.

The little fox looked a lot better this morning, dozing on a towel on Reed's lap as he watched a DVD. She sat beside him, reaching out to stroke the baby, who twitched at the touch. "How's he doing this morning?"

"Pretty well. Ate probably two ounces. And he's a she."

"Oh, that changes things." She rubbed his head softly. "Do you often rescue animals?"

He lifted a shoulder. "Done it once or twice." His expression clouded for a second. "Don't usually work out well, but she seems tough."

"Like her mother." She shivered, imagining how strong the fox must have been to try to resort to amputation to remove the trap. "Poor baby." The words were meant for the deceased mother and its offspring.

Patting his leg, she said, "Let me take over for a while, and you can sleep again."

He shook his head. "Nah, I'm fine."

She grinned. "You're a big softie."

He flushed. "Am not."

"Are too," she teased. "You're going to be a good dad."

All sign of amusement left his face. "No, I ain't."

She wet her lips, trying to tread carefully. "It's just a guess, but I'm assuming your father was...not a good dad. That doesn't mean you'd be like him."

Reed narrowed his eyes, sneering. "I ain't havin' no kids, Beth. I ain't worried about bein' like my asshole of a father. I just don't want no sniveling little bastards wreckin' my life."

"Oh." There was a burning sensation in her lungs when she drew in a deep breath. "So you don't like kids?" She'd not given it much thought, until yesterday when she'd realized she might have to in the near future, but Beth had always assumed she'd have children someday—children she wanted and loved, and who received all the attention they needed to thrive.

He shrugged. "They're all right, I suppose, but that don't make me want none. I like my life the way it is. You can't raise a family out here. I ain't in the market for kids...or a wife." There was a heavy note of warning in his tone.

Beth managed to swallow the lump in her throat, coaxing forth the cheerful mask that always saved her from revealing how deeply her father's casual rejections hurt. "Good thing little Aika came along then. She can keep you company."

His shoulders relaxed a bit, and he looked down at the sleeping fox. "Aika, huh? That's a weird name."

"I noticed last night that her eyes are about the same shade as a character on a show I've seen. At the time, I thought she was a he, so Aika was out."

Reed shrugged. "Don't matter to me what you call her."

She smirked as he stroked the fox's head. "Yeah, I can see you're unmoved." Somehow, she settled into easy chatter and companionable care of the little fox, glad he didn't realize her mask wasn't that firmly in place. What she wanted to do was curl up in a quiet, dark place until she could process that there was no future with Reed, but that was impractical. Instead, she forced herself to continue on throughout the day, taking turns napping and feeding Aika.

At the end of the day, Reed took her hand. "C'mon. We'll set the alarm and feed her when it's time. We all need some rest."

She followed him into his room, though she searched her mind for a plausible reason not to join him. Right now, she was too vulnerable to make love with him and not reveal just how much she was hurting. It was her own fault for getting in too fast and too deep, but she needed time to pull back before sharing her body with him again.

Fortunately, Aika offered a perfect excuse. She took the towel Reed offered and spread it between them, laying the fox on the makeshift blanket before lying down beside her. Aika scooted off the towel to curl up against her, resting her furry little chin on Beth's shoulder. It gave her a perfect excuse to demur if he seemed inclined, but Reed just stretched out beside her, his hand near her and the fox, and was soon asleep.

She closed her eyes, trying desperately to regroup and force away the unwanted feelings she had for Reed. Experience had taught her that it was impossible to make someone care for you if they didn't. Her dad was a perfect example. He loved her and Megan in a halfhearted way, as long as they didn't ask much from him. Beth supposed Blair loved them as much as he could, since he didn't want to put forth the effort to be a real father.

She had long ago decided she wouldn't settle for that kind of life partner, and she was determined her children wouldn't know the pain of a careless, self-involved father. While Reed had a sweet side, he didn't want kids, and she wouldn't force him to be a father. She hoped with all her might that there was no baby from her careless miscalculations, and that she could walk away from Reed without too many regrets, while retaining the larger pieces of her shattered heart.

The whimpering kit woke Reed a couple of hours later. He lifted her and cleaned her up before changing the towel. He took her for a quick trip outside, where she whined pitifully as she stood staring at him, clearly not understanding he wanted her to pee. Her sounds of distress spurred him to pick her up, and they came back inside. He warmed some of the canned milk and brought the mug and eyedropper back to the bedroom.

Aika cuddled close to him and sucked the eyedropper like a champ. It was too early to know for sure, but he'd say she had a good chance of making it. "You're a survivor, ain't ya'?" He rubbed her soft tummy that was rounding out under his hand as she drank the milk.

In one of those strange mind-jumping moments, he could suddenly see and feel his hand over a rounded human belly, belonging to Beth. The idea of her swollen with his child made him hard in an instant. It was an unashamedly male response to the idea of marking her as his woman. What better proof was there that a woman was yours than your baby in her distended abdomen?

Just as quickly, the thought soured, and he shook his head, shoving it away. He hadn't been completely honest with Beth earlier in the day. He did like kids, and maybe he might have considered having them in the past, but they didn't fit in with his plans anymore. He knew some families made this life work for their kids, but it must take love and dedication. Both parents had to want to make a life here, and he just couldn't picture Beth living in his remote cabin. Once the charm of playing house—and bedmate—wore off, she'd be chafing to get back to her coffee and Thai food life in New York City. Since she was the only woman he'd even briefly imagined as the mother of his child, and she wouldn't fit in with his life here, he didn't see children in his future.

Aika cuddled closer to him, licking his chest and making him giggle. He was embarrassed by the sound and thankful that Beth was still asleep when he stole a peek. Reed frowned at the troubled expression on her face. Leaning closer, he swore there were tear tracks on her cheeks. How many nights did the girl cry in her sleep, since she didn't allow herself to cry during the day?

Was he the cause of those tears? The thought punched him in the gut. The last thing he wanted to do was hurt her, or make her cry. He should have followed his instincts and stayed away from her. He already knew he was going to be feeling the pain for a long time after she flitted out of his life, but he'd hoped to spare her any hurt from their parting.

He frowned, doubting he was the cause of her tears. She couldn't have fallen for an ex-soldier with only a G.E.D. and no more than a few hundred dollars in his savings account at any given time, especially in just a few days. Even virgins needed more than sex to get all emotional, and he certainly hadn't given her much of anything to work with. After so many years being closed off, he wouldn't know how to open if he tried, and trying with her would be bad. She'd never be happy here, and the idea of returning to the city drenched him in a cold sweat. There was no future with Beth, beyond the few days they had in front of them.

Though he knew it would only lead to more suffering in the long run, he found himself hoping the bad weather continued for a while longer, allowing him a precious few extra days with her. Then she could go back to her real life, hopefully remembering him fondly, though probably with a hint of puzzlement as she got older, wondering what she'd ever seen in a former Georgia boy who couldn't shed his accent even in the wilds of Alaska. For him, she'd be an anomaly in his life. He was a man who preferred solitude, so he certainly wouldn't feel alone or lonely when she'd gone. Just regretful that there hadn't been a way to make it last a bit longer.

Chapter Seven

"DO YOU THINK THEY'LL actually make it through tomorrow?" asked Beth. "The weather is so capricious. We have a clear day, and then three bad ones." It had gone on like that for the past couple of weeks. Every time the sky seemed clear enough for the plane to fly, bad weather would pummel them again. She hadn't minded spending two weeks alone with Reed. In fact, she could get used to it on a more permanent basis—if he wanted that.

He nodded, taking a moment to firmly reprimand Aika for biting, though the stroke of his fingers across her muzzle softened the rebuke. "Yeah, I expect so. We've had clear weather for three days, and my pal Mike says Endline's been sunny for the past couple. The runway is shoveled on their end and ours, so they shouldn't have no trouble making it through tomorrow."

She sighed, her heart feeling heavy.

"You okay?"

Beth nodded. "Yeah, just thinking about things."

"What things?"

Oh, like the fact that I usually have cramps by now, and I haven't had a one all day. That if I don't start my period by tomorrow morning, I'm pretty positive we fucked up big time, since I've never been late. "Mainly, how things'll be when my dad gets here." *And wondering how to tell you that I made an honest mistake and try to convince you it wasn't some spoiled rich girl game to get what I wanted.*

He nodded, seemingly engrossed by Aika's never-ending cuteness.

"My dad's going to expect the guestroom."

He sniffed. "Well, there's six bunks."

"I know, but he'll barely survive a double bed in a private room. Asking him to share with the masses is beyond the pale." She rolled her eyes to indicate she was being sarcastic, in case he misinterpreted her cutting humor as sincerity.

"Guess he'll have to deal with it."

Taking a deep breath, she said, "I thought maybe I could share with you while they're shooting the documentary?" Before he could reply, she pressed on with what she'd mentally rehearsed. "I mean, I practically sleep in there every night anyway. It'd just be a matter of moving my things to your room." Without anything left to say, she fell silent, holding her breath.

Reed wore a fierce frown when he looked up. "Why?"

Opting for obtuseness, she said, "Well, my dad travels with enough luggage to mortify a diva, so he won't have room for my things in there too."

He scowled. "I mean, why do you wanna flaunt our fling? You want to punish your daddy for neglecting you by showin' him how low you can sink for attention?"

Beth flinched. "What? Of course not." How the word fling cut into her. "I'm not flaunting anything. I doubt he'd give a second thought to where I sleep or what I'm doing with my time."

Reed sneered. "Unless you give him a reason to pay attention. 'Look at the old man I'm fuckin', Daddy. See what I'm doin'.'"

She blinked back tears. "Why are you being so mean?"

"'Cause I don't wanna be part of your pageant of shame, Beth."

Her mouth tightened. "I'm not ashamed of sleeping with you. Are you embarrassed to be banging a rich girl? Do you think someone will believe I bought you? Afraid Daddy will cancel his trip and cost you some money?" She glared. "Don't worry. Even if he cared, he'd never cancel his reservation, because that would stop him from making the documentary he's creating. He has his priorities, you know," she added with mocking.

"I don't give a damn about money."

"You're full of shit."

He glowered at her. "I ain't full of nothin'. You're the one full of it, girl. You don't think your parents'd mind if they found out you was fuckin' a dirty redneck? I come from nothin', with a whore addict for a mother and an abusive alcoholic for a father. I ain't seen my sister since I was five, when our worthless mother OD'd. My father wasn't hers, so he sent her to foster care and then spent the next eleven years using me as his personal punchin' bag 'til I ran away. You ready to proclaim how proud you are of our fuckin' now, girl?"

"That was them, not you," she said quietly, trying to keep her tears in check. He wouldn't appreciate the show of sympathy and would probably mistake it for pity.

"Oh, well, let's get into me, should we? I dropped outta high school at sixteen and started stealin'. Did real good on my chosen career path 'til I got caught. It was either join the Army or go to jail, and I had ta' get my G.E.D. before I could enlist."

She shrugged, refusing to be shocked. "What difference does it make now? You're a success."

He snorted. "A success by your people's standards? I don't think so."

"I don't care about any of that—"

"Not now, but when the illicit thrill of you fuckin' the equivalent of the chauffeur wears off, you'd be humiliated. Let's be honest. There ain't nothin' for us, so there's no reason to parade our mistake in front of your dad, except to piss him off."

Heat scalded her insides, burning her lungs and down into her stomach. The sour taste of bile hovered at the back of her throat, and she suppressed it with effort. It was all a mistake to him. She'd tried to prepare herself for that attitude, having realized the day they'd discussed family that he wanted nothing from her except her body. Fool that she was, she thought she'd managed to keep her heart mostly protected and only let herself love him a little. Her stupidity really knew no bounds. Or was it her self-delusion?

Pulling back her shoulders, she did her best to transmit the genuineness of her words, wanting to leave him with the truth. "I would never be ashamed to have you by my side, Reed. Your own insecurities are speaking, not me." He scoffed, but she didn't allow him a rebuttal. "I know there is no hope for us, because that was the only option you offered from the first night I came to your bed." She managed a small smile. "Or you came to mine, I guess. You don't want a future with me, and I'm not going to stand here and try to force you to accept anything you don't want. I've spent enough time trying to make someone love me the way I need when they're never going to."

With as much dignity as she could muster, she got up off the floor in front of the fire, leaving him with the kit on his lap. "The solution to sleeping arrangements is obvious. I'm going home tomorrow when the plane lands."

"That's for the best," he snarled.

Tears clouded her eyes, but not for the reason he might have assumed. Huddled there on the floor, with only the orphaned fox for any kind of companionship, he reminded her so much of a wounded wild animal, wanting help but afraid to trust anyone offering it, that she wanted to weep for him. He was lost and alone, and though it was by his own choices, she couldn't help feeling sorry for him.

Without another word, she returned to the guestroom to pack her things, not bothering to emerge for dinner or to say goodbye. Instead, she stayed in the room and spent some time feeling sorry for herself too, because his stubbornness was costing her a future with the man she loved.

By early the next afternoon, when she walked out to meet the plane, Beth was certain she was leaving behind the man she loved and taking his child with her. After a hasty greeting from her dad, who didn't seem to care that she was cutting her trip short, she got on the plane, refusing to look back. She allowed herself one brief glimpse of Reed on the runway, wished she'd had a chance to tell Aika goodbye, and then pulled the shade.

As the plane took off a few minutes later, she allowed her thoughts to turn to the baby inside her. She wouldn't have confirmation until she took a test, but she didn't really have any doubts, knowing her own body. She supposed she should be terrified at the thought of having a baby at eighteen, without the father in the picture. Instead, she was calm, and even excited.

Finances weren't a worry, and she already knew her mother would offer emotional support, once she recovered from the shock. No one whose opinion she valued would care about her being single with a baby. She looked forward to having a piece of Reed to take with her, to hold onto. It was all of him she would ever get, so she was going to relish it. Already, she loved her baby, all the more because she couldn't love Reed, not the way she wanted. He didn't want her love, so she would lavish it on their child instead.

Patting her stomach, she said, "We'll be okay, little one." Somehow they would be, though she never would have chosen to take this journey alone.

Chapter Eight

REED STUFFED THE LAST of the supplies in the trailer behind his SUV before walking back into the general store in Endline. He'd brought the larger trailer to ensure he had room for everything, since he was a couple months later making the supply run than he should have been. It had just slipped his mind, seeming not that important the times he'd remembered he needed to make the trip. It wasn't until he'd run out of milk for Aika—who still enjoyed it as a treat in addition to her usual diet of meat, fish, eggs, and berries—that he'd forced himself to contact the store to arrange pick up of his standing order, plus some.

Hank, the old man who ran the general store, gave him a big grin when he went back to the register to settle his account, Aika his little shadow. "She's a beauty, Reed. I got all kinds of buyers for blue fox fur."

He glowered, though he knew Hank was ribbing him. "She's still got her summer coat. Ain't much value in that."

Hank laughed, shaking his head. "I'll bet she'll still be following you when her coat goes blue or white again."

Reed avoided the old man's eyes, feeling self-conscious. It was a bit strange for her to follow him around, but he couldn't have left her home alone while he made the trip. She could be mischievous and needed almost constant supervision. Plus, she would have been lonely. Not him, of course. He was used to Aika, but he wouldn't have missed her if he'd left her behind for a couple of days.

She rubbed against his calf, just like a danged cat, and he knew he was full of it. "I imagine so," he conceded as Hank ran his credit card.

As he bent to pick up Aika, wanting to keep her close in the parking lot, Hank said, "Oh, don't forget your mail, Reed."

He scooped up the bag, finding it fuller than usual—probably because he was two months late in collecting it, meaning it was eight months of mail instead of the usual six. "Guess I'm popular," he joked, making a conscious effort not to be so surly.

Hank nodded and waved him off. Reed jogged to the SUV, depositing Aika in the seat. He'd brought her favorite "blanket"—some soft sweater Beth had accidentally left in his room—and she curled up on it as he drove down four streets to the town's only lodging. It was a modest motel with four rooms on the bottom floor. The owners lived above. Since he stayed there twice a year, the female half of the couple winked at Aika and ignored the "No Pets" sign posted behind her.

After a quick meal in the café across the street, Reed gathered up his mail and headed to his room on the side of the building, Aika under his other arm. Carrying her around, he was starting to feel like one of those celebrities with their damned froufrou dogs. "The day you even think about askin' for a rhinestone collar and a sweater is the day I trade you in for a husky," he muttered to the fox as he opened the door and deposited her, along with the mailbag, on the bed.

As Aika jumped down to sniff around the queen bed and simple furnishings, he sank into the chair closest to the small round table, stretching to reach the mail and dump it out before him. He stared at the pile, feeling the overwhelming urge to shove it back in the bag and deal with it later. Only because he'd felt like that for months, and had continually put off important things when he wasn't normally a procrastinator, did he force himself to tackle the pile. Damned if he was going to turn into a moping, whining loser with a broken heart who just faded away. He'd done a good impression the past few months, but enough was enough. Beth wasn't coming back. He'd made sure of that, because it was for the best, so he didn't get to wallow in his own misery after doing the right thing.

"Man up, you little shit. You gonna cry? Yeah, go ahead, and I'll give you another'n."

The phantom sound of his dad's voice in his head, repeating that oft-heard refrain from his childhood, made Reed tense. His stomach twisted, and he forced down the surge of nausea. "That crazy drunk can't hurt me no more," he said aloud. He'd stood in front of the old man's grave when he was just twenty-two, having stopped by on leave to have the pleasure of spitting on that hallowed ground that had held such filth. He hadn't bothered to attend the funeral that had taken place six months before, and he'd never felt even a niggle of compulsion to stop by his drug addict mother's grave for a visit. Nor had he made any effort to find his sister when he'd been in the area.

That was the only thing he regretted now, looking back. At the time, he'd figured she was either as screwed up as their parents, or she'd lucked out and found a good adoptive family. He didn't want the drama of the first scenario, and he'd spared her having to acknowledge an ignorant redneck brother if she'd gotten lucky.

Maybe he'd been too hard on himself and had just decided she wouldn't want anything to do with him because of his past. Maybe she would have been pleased to see her little brother, even if they just shared a meth-head mother as their only connection. Perhaps he should look into finding her.

"Don't want to die miserable and alone," he said with a harsh laugh. Aika looked at him, head titled, as she always did when he spoke. She gave him a tentative tail wag before returning to the far more interesting task of sniffing the carpet.

With a sigh, he started sorting through his mail, separating by business and personal. All his bills were on auto-draft, so he didn't owe anything, but he'd have to keep them for his tax records. A few catalogs made the cut, since he knew there were items he'd want to order. His Internet connection at home was spotty. Controlled by satellite, it worked great on clear days, but was nonexistent the rest of the time, so he still did some old-fashioned mail ordering. He'd have to fill out his order and drop it by the general store/post office before leaving tomorrow if he wanted everything to arrive before his next trip into Endline.

An unsolicited brochure for an all-inclusive resort caught his eye, mainly because of the shapely blonde woman running across the sand. Her hair was almost the right shade to be Beth's, but of course it wasn't her. He wadded it into a ball and tossed it straight into the can before returning to sorting. Reed had almost reached the end of the pile when he discovered a stiff envelope with feminine writing he didn't recognize.

His heartbeat sped up when he read B. Wyndam in the return address. The curly cursive seemed unlikely to belong to Blair Wyndam, and why would the other man contact him anyway? Their business had concluded, he'd been paid, and that was the end of it.

Reed sat upright as he tore open the light-pink envelope, his heart galloping in his ears. A folded letter fell out, along with another, smaller envelope. On the front of the letter, she'd written "Read Me First." He unfolded it, taking a moment to drink in the sight of her elegant handwriting before allowing himself to start reading.

May 21ˢᵗ,

Dear Reed,

It seems silly to start the letter that way, but what else would I say? Anyway, I want you to know I never lied to you. I hope you'll believe that it was an honest miscalculation on my part that led to this. I really thought it was safe the night I told you to go ahead, and I didn't figure out I was wrong until several days later. I guess I should have mentioned it then, but I was afraid of your reaction, and I wanted to make sure there was something to actually worry about before I told you.

He rubbed his eyes, trying to decipher her letter. It was a bit jumbled, and he could see a couple of smeared spots that looked like tearstains. He kept reading, his stomach clenching with anxiety as he got an inkling of what he was about to discover.

I was pretty sure the day I left you that I was pregnant.

He groaned aloud, cringing when he recalled their conversation about kids.

I didn't say anything, because you made it clear you don't want children. Or a wife. At first, I hadn't planned to tell you at all, but I knew that was wrong. It's not fair to you or the baby. I owe you the chance to be included, if you want. I don't expect anything from you, and I'm not asking for anything. It was my miscalculation that caused me to get pregnant, and I release you from any obligation.

I'm writing this just after the twelfth-week ultrasound. Again, I waited to make sure I didn't miscarry, since that would have negated any need to burden you with the situation. I didn't lose it, and the midwife said everything looks fine, so I have no further reason to delay telling you. Like I said, you don't owe me or the baby a thing. I'm just trying to do the right thing by telling you, not guilting you into anything.

Beth Wyndam

P.S. The other envelope is one of the ultrasound pictures. You can't see much, and you don't have to look at all if you don't want to. I included in case you do, but it's only fair to warn you what's in there if you don't want to see it.

Reed reread the letter twice more before the information really sank in. Nausea churned in his gut, and he closed his eyes for a long moment to keep the gorge from rising.

A baby. Holy hell, he'd never expected that. Even worse was her tone, and her explicit clarity about not holding him responsible. "That's a load of crap," he said to the letter, anger surging through him. Who else was responsible, if not him? Beth couldn't bear the brunt of a baby by herself. She was too young to be a mother, let alone a single one.

His gaze fell on the other envelope, this one plain white, and his hands shook when he picked it up. He tore it open carefully, and the picture slid out easily. Reed lifted the black and white image, squinting at the blobby thing in front of him. The technician had helpfully labeled the head, arms, and legs, which made it easier to determine what was where on his child.

His child. That was like a punch in the gut. It was almost impossible to believe he was looking at the first picture of his baby. A baby he'd made with Beth. Staring down at the grainy image, an unfamiliar emotion soared through him—elation, along with a touch of awe that something so beautiful had happened without any planning on either of their parts.

Spurred on by his reaction, driven to see Beth and the baby, he picked up his cell phone and found Mike's number in the address book. After making arrangements to fly to Fairbanks the next morning, and imposing on his friend to watch Aika for a bit, he booked the next stage of his trip. It didn't take long to book a flight from Fairbanks to New York City. As he calculated the time it would take, he realized he would see Beth again in a little less than three days. Impatience made it difficult to settle down, even though he needed some sleep. He had a feeling the next few days would be exhausting, both mentally and physically.

Reed had refueled at the airport with a large coffee, getting a disdainful look from the barista when he'd declined any flavor, cream, or sweetener. "But that's just coffee," she'd protested, much to his amusement. He was glad for the extra energy, since it had been a longer walk than he'd expected. Not to mention, it was hotter than blazes outside, and he wasn't used to hundred-plus weather anymore, despite his Georgia roots.

By the time he arrived at the high-rise building that matched the address on the card Beth had sent, he was feeling tired and looked rumpled. It wasn't a surprise when the man guarding the desk gave him a suspicious look. Trying to pretend as though he belonged, and not betray his old insecurities, he said, "I'm here to see Beth Wyndam. She's on the top floor." That was just a guess on his part, but he couldn't imagine her living anywhere except the penthouse.

With narrowed eyes, the uniformed deskman lifted his phone. "Name?"

"Reed Nixon." His mouth was dry, making him wish he'd opted for water instead of coffee.

After conferring with someone on the other end of the line, the guard gestured toward the elevators. "Top floor, Suite A. Mrs. Wyndam is expecting you." He didn't bother to hide his surprise that the resident had deigned to see Reed, which made him want to slug the other man.

Reining in his temper, he hoisted his duffle bag—a leftover from his Army days—and strode to the elevator. It was like a damned movie, complete with a uniformed elevator attendant and an ostentatious gold velvet couch. He almost snorted with disgust, but held back the impulse. Foolish waste of money to impress folks.

On the top floor, the elevator attendant gave him a sunny smile as she held open the door. "Have a nice day, sir."

"Thanks." He muttered the reply as he left the cab, suddenly finding his feet dragging the closer he got to Suite A. How would Beth react to seeing him? Or Mrs. Wyndam, since it sounded like Momma Bear was the one waiting for him. Well, if she wouldn't let him see Beth, he'd just camp out on their doorstep until she relented.

He had barely rung the bell before the door opened. Reed blinked, getting a glimpse of what his Beth might look like in twenty years. The woman before him was petite and trim, with waist-length blonde hair a couple shades darker than Beth's. To his surprise, streaks of gray were visible. Her gently lined face suggested she hadn't been cosmetically altered, which was another surprise. If he'd given it much thought, he would have expected Beth's mother to be Botoxed, liposuctioned, and dyed to look fifteen years younger than her true age. Not that she looked old at all. He'd guess she was early to mid-forties, but could have passed for a decade younger on her own merits. It was uncomfortable to realize people would assume they were about the same age if they saw Reed and Mrs. Wyndam together.

Any similarity ended with her eyes. Oh, they were about the same emerald-green, but where Beth's tended to sparkle with warmth and cheer, this woman's were ice-cold, clearly denouncing him. "So, you're the bum who broke my daughter's heart."

He flinched at the accusation, but couldn't deny it. "Yes, ma'am."

"What do you want?"

He almost fumbled for the letter Beth had sent, but stopped the impulse. Despite Mrs. Wyndam leaving him feeling like a disobedient student called into the principal's office, he had to act like an adult. "I want to see Beth."

She sneered. "Why?"

"That's between me and her." Surely, her mother knew about the baby. Beth had to be showing by now, but just in case, he wasn't revealing her secret. It was her choice when to tell her mother.

She opened the door a bit wider and stepped back. "Come in."

Reed followed her inside the luxuriously appointed lair, his senses as heightened as they had been in the military and now were during a hunt. Only this time, he felt like the prey.

She stopped in the foyer, near a writing desk. Reed stood back a few steps as she wrote something. He heard a tearing sound before she stood up and turned toward him. His hand lifted automatically to accept the paper she thrust at him, and his brain didn't connect it was a check until he brought it closer. How had she put so many zeroes in that little space? "What the hell is this?"

"That's for my daughter's peace of mind. She doesn't need some loser who'll bounce in and out of her life. You take that and go."

Reed almost retorted in anger, but glancing at Mrs. Wyndam, he noticed she was watching him closely, as though evaluating him. The school pupil feeling increased, only this time, it was the same way he'd felt right before a test. After a moment, he held up the check and ripped it in half, handing it back to her. "I ain't gonna bounce anywhere, Mrs. Wyndam."

She stared at him for another minute before nodding. "It certainly took you long enough to decide to do the right thing, Mr. Nixon."

His face flushed. "It ain't no excuse for sending her away to start with, but I just got the letter about the baby. I came as quick as I could."

Mrs. Wyndam seemed to believe him, judging from her expression. With a nod, she handed him another piece of paper.

He took it cautiously, certain he wouldn't be able to hold back his anger if this was another, bigger check. Instead, it was an address. "What's this?"

"Beth's apartment. She moved into her own place last month."

He ran a hand through his hair. "Thank you for takin' care of her. I'll handle it from here."

She smiled. "I'm glad to hear it, but I didn't take care of her." At his look, she said, "I certainly would have, but there's no need. My parents left Beth her own trust, which I signed over to her after finding out she's going to be a mother." Her lips pursed. "A very young mother."

He shifted, certain he could feel a phantom needle tattooing "dirty old bastard" on his forehead in fluorescent orange. "I won't apologize for how I feel about her, but I'll admit she's too young for me."

Mrs. Wyndam surprised him with a small smile. "I know my daughter, Mr. Nixon. She's determined to have her own way, so I'd say you probably never stood a chance."

He found himself grinning. "Not really."

"One more thing. Beth told me you're a snob."

He arched a brow, shooting a glance at the priceless artwork surrounding him. The purchase price of one of those paintings would easily finance the long-term improvements he had in mind for his property. "I'm a snob?"

She waved her hand. "Toward affluence. You feel you're better than me because you've worked for everything."

"I never said that."

Mrs. Wyndam sniffed. "My daughter got the idea from somewhere that you're disdainful of wealth. It's not my place, but I want to see if you can be reasonable about her inheritance. If you insist, she'll walk away from it all and live on your earnings, but that isn't fair to her, the baby, or my parents, who wanted to ensure she had a secure future."

Reed squirmed, realizing he hadn't even given a second thought to Beth having her own money. His first inclination was to insist she let him support her, but her mother's words gave him pause. He wasn't the type of man who could ever let his wife maintain him while he sat around doing nothing, but he wouldn't deny her the funds to make her life easier. "We'll work it out."

She smiled. "Well, run along then. I'm sure you're anxious to see Beth, and if you're half the man I'm giving you credit for, we'll see each other again."

"I hope I'm at least half that man," he said. The woman was intense, but clearly loyal to her daughter. He was glad his Beth had grown up with this woman in her life, secure in the love of at least one parent, since her father was mostly absent. It sure beat the childhood he'd endured.

Reed left the high-rise, not bothering to look at the desk attendant or doorman again as he strode onto the sidewalk. He paused in a nearby doorway to use his phone to obtain a map of her apartment, pleased to find it was only a couple of blocks away.

As he covered the distance, he looked around him. The place was crawling with people, all seemingly in their best clothes, though it was a Tuesday afternoon. There were fancy cars lining the streets, along with boutiques and stores that probably cost more just to glance in their windows than he earned in a year. On the flight to New York, he'd accepted he would have to make a move back to the city, but the thought was stifling. How was he going to make it here? Would Aika adapt? At least Beth's wealth would probably make it easy enough to keep a fox in the city, without legal repercussions.

Beth groaned as she stuck her head in the freezer. It was so hot. Even the air conditioner wasn't doing much to cut through the sticky heat in the apartment. It made her miss colder weather. Deep snow. Reed...

She snorted as she grabbed a bag of frozen carrots to put on the back of her neck. It was way past time to abandon thoughts of him. After sending that letter, she'd spent a couple of weeks on tenterhooks, hoping he might call her or at least write back. In the dark of night, she'd even allowed herself the occasional fantasy of having him show up on her doorstep to sweep her off her feet.

She didn't even bother to try to generate that illusion anymore, even at her loneliest moments. He'd had to have known about the baby for at least six weeks now, so it was obvious he'd accepted her absolution of responsibility. Perhaps it shouldn't have, but it had honestly surprised her when she'd realized he'd taken the easy way out. Despite everything he'd said, she had been deluded enough to think there was still a decent man inside him, one who would want to do the right thing. What a fool she'd been.

The doorbell rang, making her curse softly. Leaving the cold of the freezer took great strength of will. She hoped it wasn't her mom or Megan dropping in to check on her. She loved them and appreciated their support, but it would be nice to have one day without one of them hovering around—especially since she was dressed in skimpy shorts and a brief camisole. Definitely not company attire, even for family.

Her heart stuttered to a stop for a brief second when she looked through the peephole and saw Reed standing on the other side. "Just a minute," she said in a scratchy voice. As she started to open the locks, she realized she still held the frozen carrots and dropped them on the foyer table.

Her hands shook as she undid the bolts and security chain, but she hoped she looked composed when she opened the door a little, not inviting him inside. "Hello." Her tone came out cool and aloof. Good girl, she praised herself.

"Uh, hi." His gaze was centered on her distended belly. An inch or so peeked out the bottom of the camisole she had stretched over the bump that morning, not bothering to find maternity clothes when she'd gotten out of the shower. It was too darned hot to go out anywhere.

He didn't say anything else, and neither did she as she resisted the urge to cover her stomach. She'd had some time to get used to it, but she was still a bit self-conscious about it. Beth wasn't sure if it was because she'd always been slender and petite, or if it had more to do with the judgmental looks and occasional snide comments she received practically wherever she went. She'd been a bit naïve to assume no one would care or say anything about a young unwed mother in the twenty-first century.

"What do you want?" she finally asked.

He looked up, his mouth slightly agape. "What'd you think, girl?"

She shrugged. "No clue."

Reed sighed, leaning against the doorjamb. Fatigue had carved lines in his face, and he looked exhausted. "Can I just come in please?"

Reluctantly, she stepped aside, moved both by his physical state and a desire to keep their private business between them. When he crossed the threshold, she closed and locked the door before walking over to a chair. She avoided the sofa and loveseat, not wanting to have him too close.

He dropped down on the loveseat next to her chair, closing his eyes for a moment and breathing deeply. "Sorry." His voice was hoarse. "Long trip."

"I'll say. At least two months," she snapped.

Reed's blue eyes opened, and he frowned. "I didn't get your letter until three days ago, Beth."

She sniffed. "It must have been delivered by sled dog."

He surprised her with a small laugh. "Just about, but it had to be sittin' at the post office a good two months waitin' for me."

"Are you blaming the postal service?" Sure, they were incompetent, but she didn't believe they'd misplaced his letter for two months.

He shook his head. "Nah, I just didn't make my bi-annual supply run on time. Kept puttin' it off so I could sit around and mope. Nothin' seemed very important after you left."

She didn't doubt his sincerity. "Oh."

Sighing, he leaned forward, elbows on his knees. "If Aika hadn't run outta milk, I'd probably still be wallowin' in self-pity and wouldn't know about the baby."

Her lips quirked at Aika's name. "I thought you were going to send her to a rehab center."

"Never got around to it. My friend said she didn't have a very good chance of being able to learn how to be a wild fox again, so she'd just be living at the facility, paraded out to folks for education." Reed lifted a shoulder. "Thought I'd spare her that."

"Where is she?"

"Endline, with my friend Mike."

Another silence settled between them, and he seemed to be searching for something to say—the right thing—as desperately as she was. "I didn't do it on purpose," she blurted out.

His gaze jumped to her stomach before going back to her face. "I didn't think you did."

Relief filled her, but curiosity made her ask, "Why not? You're not exactly the trusting type."

His lips quirked a bit. "Why would you want to trap an ol' redneck, Beth? I never doubted it was a mistake."

She straightened her spine. "Our baby was a product of a miscalculation, but she is not a mistake."

Reed held up his hand. "Whoa, girl. I didn't mean she was a mistake. I meant you gettin' pregnant. Don't think you did that on purpose. I ain't any prize. Besides, I can't imagine you doin' something so low even to catch a man worthy of you."

"Oh." That sapped some of her anger. "Thank you."

He looked at her belly again. "She? You know it's a girl for sure?"

Beth nodded. "Sorry. I guess I should have asked if you wanted to know."

Reed shrugged. "I'd rather know sooner than later. Gives me more time to prepare."

She nodded again. "Yeah." Slipping her thumb in her mouth, she began chewing on the nail, a habit she hadn't indulged in for years. "What kind of preparing do you have in mind?"

He looked a bit uncomfortable. "Well, I thought you might want to make it legal."

She arched a brow. "Was that your idea of a marriage proposal?" Talk about unromantic. Not that she should expect anything from him.

Reed tugged at the collar of his flannel shirt, which must have been scorching in the heat. "Not a formal one. Just tryin' to get your input. If you want my name for the baby, I'll give it to you."

"For the baby?" She curled her lips, glaring at him. "I don't need your name for the baby. I don't need anything from you."

"Hell, I know that," he shouted, getting to his feet. "Your momma told me you're all set with your trust fund." He paced, dragging a hand through his hair. "I know you don't need nothin' from me, Beth, so why'd you send the letter? If you don't want me here, why'd you tell me about the baby?"

She softened her voice, striving to remove the simmering anger. He was making an effort. "I didn't say I don't want you here. I just don't want anything from you out of obligation."

He waved at her stomach. "That's a pretty big obligation there, Beth."

Tears came to her eyes, and she sniffed. When she replied, it was with a fair bit of her own shouting. "I released you. I want you to be here because you want to be, not because you feel like you should be."

He froze. "I didn't mean it that way. You ain't forcing me to be here. I came 'cause my baby's growing in your belly, and I want to be here with you."

"Oh." She sniffed away the rest of the urge to cry. "Well, what do you want to happen? What do you need?"

"I don't know. I'd just sort of planned to give you whatever you asked for."

Beth rolled her eyes. "You can be so frustrating at times, Reed Nixon."

He gave her a small grin. "I'm willin' to concede that point."

"Okay, I'm asking you to tell me one thing you want. Let's start with that."

He hesitated, his gaze on her stomach. "I'd like to feel your stomach and see the changes."

Beth's eyes widened. That wasn't what she'd expected, since they'd been discussing practicalities. In the spirit of compromise, she couldn't really refuse or try to redirect, since he'd met her terms of expressing one thing he wanted. "Um, okay." Feeling reluctant, she got to her feet and slid the camisole up under her unfettered breasts.

He came closer, his hands trembling a bit when he rested them on her stomach. "You're bigger'n I expected." She flinched, making him frown. "Did I hurt you?"

Beth shook her head. "No, but those aren't the best words to say to a fat, frumpy pregnant woman."

He scowled. "You ain't fat. That's a baby in there. My baby." He purred the last two words, leaving no doubt he was staking a claim. "You're beautiful, Beth."

She sniffed again, hating the hormones that left her on perma-drip. "I don't feel very beautiful these days, Reed. I have eyes."

"Then use them. Where's a mirror?" He took her hand, tugging her along behind him until they came to her bedroom. Snapping on the light, he led her right to the mirrored door that extended the length of the closet. With impatient movements, he stripped off her camisole, putting his hand on her stomach. "This is beautiful." He touched her face with his other hand. "Still beautiful. Maybe even more beautiful. You got a glow, girl."

She blushed, inexplicably shy, though unable to tear her gaze from his hands in the mirror. The one on her tummy splayed wider, encompassing most of her bump.

"You have any idea what it does to me to know my baby is in you?" He stepped closer behind her, his erection poking into her lower back. "It's sexy as hell. Ain't real modern to say, but it gives me a thrill to know I marked you as mine. You're my woman, and this bump—our baby—tells the world you're mine."

Hypnotized by his words and his hands, she watched/felt the one on her face moving lower, to stroke her neck. "Mine," he said again, softly, as his hand slipped lower. She held her breath, tummy fluttering, as he cupped one of her swollen breasts, touching the nipple with exquisite gentleness that made heat flare inside her.

"Mine." He thumbed the nipple. "Until it's hers." He patted her tummy. "Thinkin' of your breasts doin' what they were meant to, producin' milk for my baby...I ain't got words for it, Beth."

Tears swam in her eyes, and she leaned back against him as he rubbed her tummy for another minute before putting both hands around the bump. "This is mine. You belong to me, Beth, and I was a damned fool not to see it sooner."

She lifted a hand behind her, to tangle in his hair. "It goes both ways. If I'm yours, you're mine too. That means you have to stop worrying about if you're good enough or too old. None of that matters. Only you matter."

He buried his face in her neck. Even as his lips feathered over the delicate skin, she swore she felt moisture from his eyes. Soon, his teasing kisses distracted her from anything but the sensations coursing through her body, and she didn't protest when he picked her up to carry her to bed.

He laid her down, his magical hands somehow managing to make her shorts disappear in the process. It had been too hot for underwear, so she lay nude before him as he shucked off his clothes. "Gotta get some city outfits," he commented, as he came down beside her.

"Or just stay inside, naked."

His eyes gleamed with interest. "That's a fine idea too, as long as you're plannin' to join me."

His mouth on hers stole her ability to respond, so she threaded her fingers through his hair to drag him closer. It had been too long since they'd touched or kissed. Her body hadn't forgotten. She'd been on a slow simmer, but that fire blasted to a raging inferno at first contact, especially when his fingers slipped between her thighs to stroke her slick folds.

When he held up his fingers, her arousal glistened. "You're so wet." He sounded awed.

"Your fault," she managed to say as he swept his tongue across her tongue and down her chin. A few seconds later, his mouth found her nipple, and she dug her heels into the mattress, crying out. "Oh, god, that hurts, but in a good way."

He lifted his head, frowning. "You want me to stop?"

She shook her head. "It's just so sensitive now."

Reed dipped his head, gentling his tongue as he traced it around her nipple before moving to the other to offer some attention. "They're bigger."

She nodded shyly. "About a cup size."

He grasped one in his hand, squeezing carefully. "Love it. You was perfect before, but there's something that drives me wild about your fertile little body right now. Can't wait to see how big they get." He squeezed again.

Scooting lower, he parted her legs, bringing his face close to inhale. "You smell different too." With an air of experimentation, he lowered his head to run his tongue down her slit before looking up. "You taste different too. Sweeter, with a bit of spice." He lapped her again, catching the rivulets that ran from her lips. "I could eat your pussy all day, Beth."

She moaned as he darted his tongue inside her before taking a slow stroke. "I just want you inside me, Reed. Please, just fuck me."

He sat up, moving to lie beside her with his back propped against the pillows piled in front of her headboard. "I ain't gonna fuck the mother of my child. I'm gonna make love to you."

Her chest felt tight, and she had to draw in a deep breath to regain composure. "You're a true romantic."

With a laugh, he lifted her onto his lap, her back to his chest, both of them facing the mirror. "It's my downfall." Burying his hand in her ponytail, he pulled her head back a bit while aligning the head of his cock against her soaking pussy. "You feel how hot you're makin' me?" His cock slid inside her, burying to the hilt with no resistance. He groaned and stilled, as though savoring the sensation. "God, you feel real good around me, Beth." When she tightened her muscles, he groaned again. "Just like that, baby. Squeeze me and ride me."

Slowly, Beth lifted off him, trying to keep her sheath clenched around him, before sliding down again. It was heaven, riding his cock. The ridge of his erection hit her walls just right, making her cry out and grind against him. She rocked faster as he dug his fingers into her hips and started thrusting against her, almost slamming his cock inside her.

"Damn, I missed you, Beth. Missed this." He rocked against her hard, maintaining pressure against her g-spot as they stilled for a moment. "Mostly, I just missed you."

She nodded, incapable of speech as she thrust against him, wanting release so badly. His cock was hard and almost punishing, but it felt so good that she didn't care if she walked funny for a week afterward.

As his cock tightened before convulsing, he put his hands on her stomach again, holding her against him as he came, while he said with savage delight, "Mine."

The bunched chords in his neck, the fiercely possessive expression, and the hot spurts of his satisfaction all served to bring Beth crashing into an orgasm that left her shaking and moaning his name. Afterward, she slumped backward, moving with him when he lowered her to the mattress and turned so they were lying side by side, faces almost touching.

"Did you mean it?" She bit her lip. "That 'mine' stuff?"

He nodded. "Yeah. There ain't never been anyone before for me. Not like this, Beth. I ain't never had a girlfriend or any kind of real relationship."

She frowned. "But you're thirty-three. How is that possible?"

He shrugged. "I didn't want the baggage. I've had fuck-buddies and plenty of one-night stands, but I ain't never...cared about anyone until you."

She longed for words of love, but knew it was too soon. As closed as Reed was, she might never get the actual words, but it didn't matter. As long as he showed her in other ways, she could be okay with that. "I haven't either."

He smirked a bit. "Of course you ain't. You're about a second old, girl." Reed's face clouded. "Someday, you'll change your mind." He said it with enough conviction to hurt, because he obviously believed it.

Beth shook her head. "I won't. It wouldn't matter if I'd met you when I was eight or eighty, instead of eighteen. I'd still have fallen for you." Allowing a little of her pain to show, she said, "Frankly, I'm insulted that you think I'm just so fickle that I can fall in and out of love like that. I'm not my father."

Reed winced. "I know that, baby. I didn't mean to hurt you. Just tryin' to be realistic."

She glared. "You're being an ass. I already told you that you have to stop doubting your worth to me. I'm never going to love anyone the way I love you."

He closed his eyes, looking like he was torn between agony and hope. "I'm going to do my best to believe that, Beth. It ain't that I doubt you. I just don't see why you'd want to be with me." Cupping her stomach, he said, "If I didn't knock you up, you wouldn't be stuck with me."

Beth rolled her eyes. "I'm not stuck with you. I wanted you, and I went after you. I'm not a cheating whore, like my father, but I am a determined woman used to getting my own way." Putting a hand on his cheek, she softened her tone. "Unlike my dad, when he gets what he wants, I don't get bored and move on. If this relationship fails, it will be because you leave me, not the other way around."

He frowned. "I ain't gonna leave you, girl." Apprehension shadowed his blue eyes. "Not sure what I'm gonna do here in the city, but I ain't leaving you."

It was her turn to frown."What do you mean, here in the city? We're going back to Alaska."

He snorted. "You can't go back there with a kid on the way."

Beth gritted her teeth. "I know for a fact they have midwives and doctors in Alaska. They tend to be everywhere."

He arched a brow. "For a fact, huh? How?"

Her cheeks warmed. "I might have done a little Googling after I mailed you the letter. I kind of hoped you'd want me to come back." Putting her hand over his on her stomach, she squeezed. "I believed you were a decent man and would want some part in the baby's life, even if you didn't want me."

"I never stopped wantin' you, Beth. I sent you away 'cause I know I ain't good enough for you." He held up a hand before she could protest.

"In my heart, I know I ain't, but I'm going to try to make you happy and be what you need."

She narrowed her eyes. "Is that because you want to, or because you feel obligated?"

His eyes widened. "I want to. I want to be there for you and the baby. It'll take me a bit of time to find a buyer for the Alaskan property, and to figure out what the hell I'm gonna do with myself in New York City, but I'm hopin' to have that all settled by the time she's born."

She frowned. "And what about Aika? Are you just going to forget about her?"

He frowned. "'Course not. She'll fit right in, already practically a damned froufrou dog as it is." A grin lightened his expression. "I can see her strutting down the street in one of those soft pink sweaters like you wear, with a diamond collar."

Beth giggled, but shook her head. "No, her home is in Alaska. So is yours. So is mine."

He shook his head. "I ain't riskin' your life and health to have a baby in the middle of nowhere."

"Honey, I'm rich." She blushed. "I'm not bragging, but I'm simply pointing out that money buys things that makes life easier—like having my midwife come stay with us for the last month or so before the birth, if it makes you more comfortable. We'll make it work."

He frowned. "You shouldn't have to make it work. I can't ask you to give up coffee and Thai food."

Beth laughed. "That was a silly throwaway comment, Reed. I can make coffee and learn how to cook Thai food. Don't you get it? I was happy there. Happier than I've ever been anywhere. Mostly, that was because of you, but I also liked the land and the environment. I want the life we can have there."

After a moment of hesitation, he asked, "You sure you ain't just sayin' that to make me happy?"

"I don't lie." Keeping her expression firm, she said, "You might as well know I'm not budging on this. If you're determined to stay in the city, you can have my apartment, but I'm going back to Alaska."

Reed pulled her closer for a long kiss. "I'd follow you anywhere, girl."

"Then follow me home."

Epilogue

BETH CAME OUT OF THE bathroom, drying her hair on a towel. She smiled at the sight of Reed standing in front of the window of their bedroom with Kerri tucked against his chest. He wore just his boxers, and the baby was in her diaper, so he was obviously about to give her a bath.

She walked over to her family, kissing her daughter on the forehead before getting a long kiss from her husband. "Sorry if she woke you. I'd hoped to slip in for a quick shower while she was asleep, before she wanted to nurse."

"It's no problem. She's a morning gal, like her momma, but I can handle it."

"As long as you have coffee," she teased.

"With milk." He squeezed her breast playfully.

Beth rolled her eyes, holding out her arms for the baby. Kerri flailed her arms and threw herself forward, saying, "Milk."

"You two are so alike." She carried their daughter to the rocker, untied her robe, and let the baby latch. "Mom called to confirm she and Megan will arrive next month for the celebration. Megan's bringing some family too. Have you heard from your sister? Is she definitely coming for Kerri's birthday party?"

He nodded. "Marlie confirmed and said Lila was comin' too."

Lila was his niece, and he'd been a little discomfited to learn she was a year older than Beth, though Beth hadn't cared. Reed was almost to the point that he didn't stop and chastise himself for robbing the cradle every few days, but he still had moments where he couldn't understand what she saw in him. Beth was pleased that he always told her when he was having doubts.

Wearing a bit of a frown, he walked over to the bed to sit near them. "It took a bit of convincin' to let us pay her way."

She smiled, liking "us." When she'd first converted all her accounts to joint access, he'd still called it her money. It had taken him several weeks to use even a penny of it, and he'd clearly wanted to protest when she'd found his expansion plans and started setting up appointments with builders and suppliers. Still, he'd given in as graciously as he could, and they now had a separate building for housing clients, a better airstrip, more modern equipment, and a completely self-contained power supply that didn't rely on the public utility service.

Their cabin was basically the same, though they'd knocked out a couple of walls and turned the guest quarters into a bedroom suite and adjoining nursery. Now that she was older, Kerri slept in her own crib most nights, where faithful little Aika acted as her guard, having taken to shadowing the baby instead of Reed. The two girls were inseparable. "You know, I was thinking..."

He groaned.

She frowned at him. "What?"

Reed lifted a shoulder. "The last time you said that, you told me you'd found a private investigator who was ready to find my sister."

"I knew you'd been thinking about it, but sometimes, you need a bit of prodding." Beth smiled. "And that's turned out beautifully."

"Yeah, but what about the plane? I still can't get the hang of flyin' it."

That had been an impulsive gift she'd given him. It had occurred to her that they should have a plane they could both fly, in case of an emergency. Their instructor flew in twice per week. So far, Beth was acing everything, but Reed had been a little less confident and was having some difficulty mastering the task. She found it endearing that he kept at it with dogged determination, though he got frustrated during every lesson.

"Oh, you know I'm full of good ideas."

"Full of somethin'," he muttered, but there was a gleam of interest in his gaze when he looked at her bared breast that Kerri hadn't latched onto yet. "Could make you full of something else too, once she goes down for a nap."

Beth chuckled, her body tingling at just the thought of making love with her husband. He could drive her crazy with just a look. "Would you like to know what I was thinking?"

"Sure, honey."

"It occurs to me that you must feel a bit outnumbered with all the girls in the house—me, Kerri, and Aika."

He lifted a shoulder. "Don't bother me none."

"Maybe we should get a dog. A big boy named Rex." She'd just happened to see a malamute-mix on the Fairbanks animal shelter's website the night before, coincidentally named Rex...

Reed shrugged. "I don't see no harm in addin' to the family." The hunger that abruptly flared in his gaze sent a rush of need through her. "Matter of fact, I been thinkin' too."

"Oh?"

"Kerri's going to need brothers and sisters, living all the way up here. There ain't any neighbor kids."

She nodded. "That's true."

"I was thinkin' we should start tryin' again soon."

Beth smiled. "Funnily enough, I was thinking the same thing early this morning, when I was nursing Kerri after she woke up for a diaper change." She tilted her head. "It could take a few months, you know, since I'm still breastfeeding."

He lifted his shoulder. "Ain't no rush, and it sure ain't a hardship to keep tryin'."

She giggled. "I love the idea."

Reed's expression turned serious, and he picked up her left hand, his finger rubbing across the plain gold band there. "And I love you, Beth. I don't say it near enough, but I do."

She turned her hand to squeeze his. "I know, honey. You show me every day. I don't need the words."

He blushed. "You might not need 'em, but I need to say 'em. I like hearing you tell me you love me, so I imagine you feel the same?" At her nod, he said again, "I love you."

She leaned forward to meet his mouth, whispering against his lips, "Love you too," before he kissed her. It was a mark of possession they bestowed upon each other, leaving no doubt they belonged with, and to, each other.

If you enjoyed this story and would like to receive notifications of new releases or access bonus chapters for your favorite books, please join my Mailing List[1]. You'll also receive six books just for joining—and I'll tell you how to read my books before anyone else, and for less! If you prefer to receive notifications for just one, or a few, of my pen names, you'll have the option to select which lists to subscribe to at signup.

---

1. http://kittunstall.com/newsletter/

About Kit Kyndall

Kit Kyndall is the pen name *USA Today* bestselling author Kit Tunstall uses when writing contemporary erotic romances. It's simply a way to separate the myriad types of stories she writes so readers know what to expect with each "author."

Join Kit's Mailing List[1] **to keep up with new releases and receive exclusive content.**

---

1. http://eepurl.com/bpdvb9

Did you love *Snowbound*? Then you should read *A Royal Pain*[2] by Kit Kyndall!

A playboy prince Bennet Casparian was once a hard-partying, racing, playboy prince until he wrecked his racecar and ended up paralyzed. Now, he's wounded and angry with the world. The last thing he needs or wants is some know-it-all American pushing him to recover—especially the dowdy woman his doctor recruits for the task. But if she's so plain, why can't he stop thinking about her?**A stubborn physical therapist**Harper is happy with her job at the VA, but irresistibly tempted by her ex-fiancé's job offer to rehabilitate an injured (and spoiled) Montrovian prince. He's already driven away two physical therapists, but she's determined to stick it out.**An unexpected connection**He pushes her buttons and tries to keep her away, but she

2. https://books2read.com/u/3k0vvW

3. https://books2read.com/u/3k0vvW

finally breaks through his resistance. The more time she spends with him, the more she wants the prince, and the attraction is definitely mutual. Their relationship is forbidden for many reasons, so why does it feel so right?**An unforeseen consequence**They've broken the rules, and it's only a matter of time until someone finds out. When their secret comes to light, Harper might lose everything important to her—including Bennet.

Also by Kit Kyndall

Kingwood Prep
Catching His Eye

Protectors
Safe Harbor
Hart & Soal

Pure Escapes
Ablaze
Out Of Bounds
Guarded
Succumb
Taking
Proposition
I'm No Saint Nick

Sage Valley
Reunion

A Second Chance

Seen
Catching His Eye, Part 1
Catching His Eye, Pt. 2
Catching His Eye, Pt. 3

SpicyShorts
Pawn
Two Cowboys for Cady
Ebony Enigma
Wrong Groom
Model Behavior
Biology Lessons
Mai Tais on the Beach
All Grown Up
SpicyShorts Bundle

Sweet Escapes
Falling For A Firefighter
Worth Waiting

Well...
Well-Seasoned

www.ingramcontent.com/pod-product-compliance
Lightning Source LLC
Chambersburg PA
CBHW070842160726
48004CB00001B/476